PROMISED TO ME
A COLLEGE MAFIA ROMANCE
SHANA COLLINS

PolyPen Publishing

DEDICATION

For all the dedicated mafia romance readers who loves a bad boy
in a black suit with his hand around your throat.

NOTE TO READERS

Promised to Me is a college mafia romance full of violence, lust, and heartbreak.

This book is the prequel to Deadly Decisions, the first book of the Savin Brothers Bratva series, but can be read as a standalone.

This book contains violent and spicy romance scenes that may not be suitable for all readers. 18+ only.

Contents

CHARACTERS

Andrei Savin- Future Brigadier, eldest Savin brother, Vice-President of all Savin family businesses

Cora Belov- Future wife of Andrei through arranged marriage

Sasha Belov- Cora's twin brother, best friend and second-in-command to Andrei Savin, future leader of Belov family business

Mr. Savin- Brigadier, the Savin brothers father

Mrs. Savin- The Savin brothers mother

Dmitri Savin- Second-eldest Savin brother

Nikolai Savin- Third-eldest Savin brother, part of the Coalition's army

Anton & Alexi Savin-Twins, the youngest Savin brothers

The Pakhan- The Savin brother's uncle, leader of the Coalition

Mr. Belov- Cora and Sasha's father, head of the Belov family business

Mrs. Belov- Cora and Sasha's mother

Valentin Volkov- Coalition Brigadier and Andrei's Godfather, Coalition's arms dealer

The Professor- Expert in natural resources, business partner to Andrei

Adam- Cora's college boyfriend

Nicole- Cora's college roommate

Michael- Cora's personal security guard while at college

Chapter One

CORA BELOV

FRESHMAN YEAR

It's only been a month since I left Seattle, only to return a different woman. A woman- no longer an untouched girl saving herself for marriage.

Cherry blossoms twirl through the streets, caught in the wind. I feel a sense of excitement as I breathe in their heady scent, that same feeling I had when I stepped onto campus for the first time during the fall semester.

But now, winter break is over. As the thousands of blossoms fall onto the ground and go tripping by on the next gust of air, I have a saddening realization that my sense of renewal and my innocence are both gone.

I'm still surprised that my parents even agreed to let me attend college across the country.

I had worked so hard during high school to ensure I got the best grades and college recommendations, specifically so that when the time came, I could escape New York City and stand here in Seattle with all the hope of new possibilities.

I started the fall semester with a feeling of independence as I embarked on my new college experience away from my family and the Coalition. By now, I have made new friends and even started dating Adam, the charming basketball captain.

He's my first boyfriend, as I wasn't ever allowed to date in high school. My father didn't want to see or even hear about any boys at all, his face reddening as if his blood pressure had shot sky-high at the merest whisper of the male sex.

Just a month ago, I left campus with hopes and dreams. Yet now, I return from winter break with apprehension about what I truly want, overwhelmed with this whirlwind of thoughts.

All I can think of is *him.*

No, it's not my boyfriend. It is Andrei Savin. He wanted my innocence, and I gave it to him willingly and maybe a little too quickly, as if I just couldn't wait. No hesitations, not even a 'no.'

It's been six months since I last saw him. I remember how he handed me a white rose and said goodbye the day before I left for college. *Was that supposed to be an official goodbye?* After all, he would attend New York University near his family and the Coalition.

A man like Andrei can choose what university he wants to attend. His family is Russian mafia royalty, and he's the heir to the throne. Yes, he can go anywhere and study anything since every university would want him. Or maybe they just don't dare to decline.

We grew up together, our lives intertwined, and our families well acquainted. Our fathers still work together, but Andrei has never considered me a friend. Instead, he's always hung out with his siblings, the famous Savin brothers, and his best friend and second-in-command, Sasha.

They ruled our schools. They ruled the Coalition. They *still* do. You can say that they ruled New York City, even.

I was just the quiet girl sitting in the corner reading a book, fantasizing about fleeing the city and my father and wishing I were living in another reality.

But he was always staring, always watching me. It felt as if he was my protector, my knight, even though we only hung out with each other because our families were acquainted. So, I never understood why every year since I was a little girl, I would receive white roses for my birthday with a card only signed 'Andrei.' Sweet but confusing. It still is.

We are nothing alike. Yet, he has left an imprint on my life and marked my heart. During my visit back home, he awoke in me a thirst for something. Something wicked and addicting. Something from which I might never be able to free myself!

Walking into the Pakhan's Christmas Eve party, I was more confident than the girl who had left for college.

I immediately noticed him standing across the room, exhibiting confidence and power. Over six feet tall with a prominent jawline and the most beautiful eyes, Andrei knew how to stand out in a crowd. He appeared as the devil in an expensive suit, the evil that everyone knew in one way or another.

That night that changed everything!

***

A look of surprise crossed his face as I stepped into the center of the room.

It had been six months since anyone had seen me. In Seattle, where I was just me, the girl from New York, I gained confidence in who I was as a person, not the Mafia princess I'd been raised to be.

To my surprise, he didn't look away. No, he stood there glaring at me for what seemed like a long time, but it must have been only a few minutes before he headed toward me. "I see you came home from Seattle."

"Yeah, it's winter break," I replied, now perplexed that he was even talking to me alone in a room full of people. His question was odd, like he was trying to make small talk but was doing it very poorly.

"Do you like Seattle?" He sipped his wine slowly, staring at me as if I was his next meal. I couldn't help but stare at his lips. For years, I had been dreaming of those lips on mine.

"Yes. I do." Now, I was the one sounding silly. But he did ask.

I smiled back and looked around the room, noticing that every woman in that place was staring at me, envious that I had Andrei's attention. The thought gave me chills.

"What do you like about it?" he asked, genuinely interested in knowing about me and my life there.

"It's gorgeous there." It's not entirely a lie. But I wouldn't divulge my reason for running to Seattle, which was to get away from my father and the physical pain he'd been causing me my whole life. I had the scars to prove it.

"Maybe I should visit sometime if it's that good," he teased me.

I didn't know what to say, so I stood there, immediately regretting my appearance tonight. Why would a man like Andrei waste his time visiting me in Seattle? Why, after all this time, was he showing an ounce of interest now that I was miles away?

Taking another sip of wine, he hid his grin as though he liked teasing me. His gaze glittered, making my body quiver as heat rushed to the surface of my skin.

"I'll see you before you leave," he said it as though it wasn't even a question.

Before I could answer, he leaned in close, gently took a strand of my hair, and pulled it behind my ear.

I felt my heart seem to stop, then speed up. I didn't know what I felt, but it was something like anxiety and excitement all at once. The only thing I knew for sure was that my panties had gotten completely wet from just the touch of his finger.

In an effort to catch my breath, I took a moment to look away, finding everyone's eyes watching the two of us, including our parents.

***

"Welcome home, babe." My body tenses at the sudden noise.

"Hi," I yelp loudly, mustering a faint smile, pulling myself away from my thoughts.

"How was your winter break in New York?" Adam brings me into a hug, too close for comfort when my thoughts have been far from him.

"Boring. I just read some books," I say with a fake smile as though I'm happy to see my supposed boyfriend, the one I haven't even spent time thinking about. Shrugging, I grab his hand and walk toward my dorm room.

When I met Adam the first week of college, he was different from any man I'd grown up with. He's fun and makes me laugh. I hesitated initially because I wasn't sure how much I liked him, but I decided to give him a chance after his persistence.

But our relationship does not extend beyond our superficial college life here. He's not from my world. He doesn't understand me and never will.

Our walk to my dorm room is odd and long. I give the many girls watching us a quick wave as I pass by. They wave back, barely noticing me, their eyes on the basketball captain walking next to me. But it doesn't bother me, probably because I know deep in my heart there will be no future with Adam.

A rumbling starts in my stomach when we approach my room, number 403.

"I'm tired from all the traveling," I cut in, standing on my tiptoes to kiss his cheek. Before he offers to come in, I add, "See you in class tomorrow."

I try to shut the door quickly, but Adam is just as persistent. He wedges his hand around the edges, stopping the door from closing. "I have time to come in for a few minutes," he says.

"Not tonight," I tell him, trying not to hurt his feelings but desperately wanting some alone time away from everyone. He looks hurt and bewildered, pulling his fingers out of the doorway. He steps back. With a hard push, the door shuts, almost slamming into his face.

Suddenly, I find peace in the quietness of my room, but the knot in my stomach gets bigger. I throw my jacket and purse on my desk and walk over to my bed.

My blood runs cold, and my skin turns gray when I see what's waiting for me. In the middle of my bed lies a single white rose and a note with only one word- *Kitten*.

Chapter Two

ANDREI SAVIN

Cora walked into the Pakhan's party head high, confident, and breathtaking as ever. When I first saw her that evening, a sigh escaped my mouth. How had the girl I had known growing up become a woman during her time away? She was undeniably beautiful, and I had to delve into my pants and adjust my cock under my black suit.

I couldn't keep my eyes off her. She wore a tight black dress that fell right above her knees. Her figure tall and skinny, with long brunette hair falling down her back. During high school, when the city girls grew old enough to wear too much makeup and shorter dresses, Cora always maintained a classic look. She dressed like old money, wearing a sophistication that came with her upbringing.

No longer the girl sitting in the corner reading her book, she stood in the middle of the room holding a glass of wine, engaging in conversation. My gaze immediately went to her lips. Something about them that evening made me want to touch them. Perhaps the red lipstick reminded me of an apple waiting to be bitten into. Every so often, she would lick them, and my cock would twitch again.

I glanced around the room and noticed I wasn't the only one watching her. Other men were also mesmerized by her beauty. My murderous glare met each of them, and their eyes darted elsewhere instantly.

Leave her alone, my mind warned me. *She's not ready for the life you have planned for her.*

But seeing her that night made that difficult. Not having her in my life for the last six months had also caused a pain in my heart that neither she nor I could have imagined. So, I started walking over to her, oblivious to anyone watching, not even caring if they were. It's as though my heart was gravitating to her soul, and I couldn't stop it, simply powerless.

I rambled like a stupid, silly schoolboy, and before I could walk in the opposite direction, I made the mistake of touching her. Just a strand of her hair made me want more, and I found myself unable to stay away from my Cora.

***

As the party started winding down, I found myself standing outside of Cora's door. I knocked softly.

"Come in." As I turned the knob and opened the door, I could hear footsteps walking toward me.

An innocent Cora stood in front of me, wearing a pink camisole that allowed me to see her nipples through the lace.

"Sorry, I thought you were my mom." She hid her body behind her folded arms.

"You looked beautiful tonight." I stepped further into her room, closing the door behind me.

"Thank you," she said with a faint smile, then stepped back, retreating away from me.

"Seattle seems to make you happy," I admitted with guilt. I'm still not sure why I came to see her. But I also knew why, and it was because my cock had been

aching since seeing her earlier. I'd only thought about those wet red lips giving me a release since I'd first laid eyes on them.

"Yes," she confirmed, tilting her head down, embarrassed to be standing in front of me half-naked. But I was enjoying the view.

"When you're done with college, you will return to New York, right?" I asked, knowing she was bound to me and would have no choice.

I moved closer to her. Close enough that I felt my skin against hers and her breath on my neck.

"Yes, that's the plan," she responded with a half-smile. Her wandering eyes were telling me a different truth.

"You wouldn't be lying to me, would you?" I ran my finger down her cheek as my gaze dropped to her lips. I had a deep desire to bite them.

"I'm not sure. Maybe if there's something worth coming home to."

Her eyes gave me a pleading look, the same one she had always given me when she craved my attention. She stepped back, away from me. I watched her chest rise and fall as she stood nervously.

I grabbed her arm and pulled her into me, my erection pressing against her stomach. "You can come home to me," I told her sternly and commandingly.

"Andrei!" she gasped, surprised.

I reached down and kissed the pair of sultry lips I craved. My desire was so thick that my cock extended when I felt her wetness seeping through her panties and onto my pants.

She placed her hands on my chest. "Andrei, we can't." She tried to pull away from me.

I kissed her harder, confessing, "Cora, you belong to me. You're mine."

***

Since we were kids, I delivered a bouquet of white roses to her home for her birthdays. I don't know why I started doing it. I remember as a young boy how my mother would smell the roses my father sent, and they would instantly make her smile. It was my way of claiming her as mine without uttering a single word.

White roses represented loyalty, purity, and innocence all that my Cora is or once was. But that night, in her room, the crimson stains we left on her sheets transformed everything. I became the darkness that tainted her innocence.

That night everything changed. That was the moment I knew for sure Cora had become mine in body and soul. I couldn't let her return to Seattle and forget about me and her place next to me. So, it was time to collect a debt owed to me. Payment had fallen due!

I look around my surroundings, and it no longer feels like home. Where New York City is an impressive place that bleeds money, I'm now in a charming town that smells of misty rain. *Oh Seattle, it's been a long time my old friend.*

"Mr. Savin, here's your class schedule. Welcome to the university." The older lady in the office hands me a piece of paper. I look at it and make sure all the suitable classes are on it. I'll be majoring in business since I'm already the vice-president of various U.S. and Russian entities.

I step onto the sidewalk and look at the delicate trees that drop the purest white and pink flowers at my feet, their fragrance perfuming the air. The cherry blossoms remind me of her, and I know I've made the right decision to come here.

I take a deep breath and smile. Placing my hands in my pocket, I stroll down the sidewalk, making my way to Room 403.

Chapter Three

CORA

After a cold and windy walk through the center of the university, I finally reach the business building, staring at it before walking in. I'm already annoyed.

I wanted to major in literature and writing to become an author one day. I love books and stories, taking my imagination to utterly incredible worlds. My perfect afternoon is sitting under a tree or in the corner of the library and reading a good book. I'm a sucker for romances. The fictional men in the stories give me hope there are still men out there who are loving and would sweep me off my feet.

But my father, of course, had other plans.

One of the stipulations of attending the university is that he got to pick my major, so here I am, on my way to attending my first Business 101 class. The Coalition runs on business deals and money, so Father insisted I needed to understand capitalism, competition, and finances. I can still hear his lecture as I pick out my classes.

After some begging, I finally got him to reluctantly agree for me to attend a few writing classes as my electives.

The halls are filled with chatter and the smell of coffee on the first day of the semester. The campus is back to its busy self after the silence the winter break had brought to us all while we were enjoying our time at home. After being in New York, I returned a few days early to enjoy some alone time, read, and gather my thoughts. But it feels as if I haven't even been away.

I enter the classroom, and already, the first two rows of seats are taken, so I head toward the back and grab a seat in the second to the last row. I take a deep breath and sip my coffee, still feeling weird and slightly anxious since finding a white rose on my bed.

Still, Andrei is in New York City, so instead of pining for him, I must focus on the semester ahead of me. I open my laptop and get ready for class to start.

However, the class silence brings my mind back to him and the night that began with a kiss.

***

When he kissed me, my heart melted. I had been imagining Andrei and me since we were in high school, but my imagination was nothing close to this moment. Now, here was that long-awaited moment, and I scarcely dared breathe in case it was all a dream.

His hands wandered down my arms and ended on my ass. I felt his large fingers fold under my ass cheeks, squeezing as he kissed me harder.

My mouth opened wider as a moan quietly escaped me. "Andrei."

He pressed his finger on my lips as he moved his mouth down my chin, neck, and chest. His muscular arms grabbed my legs as he lifted me in the air, wrapping my legs around his waist and pinning them there.

As he pulled my hair, my head fell backward, and he placed his lips on my camisole, his wet tongue licking and sucking my hardened nipples. I clenched my thighs tightly, trying to ease the sensation vibrating through my middle. I had never felt an ache like this before.

He quickly threw me on the bed. It startled me, and I giggled. I had always thought his arms were muscular, but feeling him throw me like a doll heightened my excitement. I licked my lips in anticipation of what was to come when he slowly moved to the bed, crawling on top of me like a predator, momentarily pinning my arms back behind my head before letting them go free.

"Cora," he whispered as he continued to rub a hand up and down my body. When did my name become so sexy?

I wrapped my arms around his head and pulled him deeper into me, kissing him hard and exhaling a deep breath.

His hands slid the strings of my camisole off my arms before he lifted it over my head, bearing my chest to him.

His mouth slowly attached to my nipples, first the left, then the right, nibbling and sucking on them, my pink nipples erect with excitement.

He moved his head to my middle and kissed me from the bottom right up to my clit, flicking his tongue against the magic spot barely hidden behind the sheer fabric of my underwear before he pulled my panties down my legs. The anticipation had me dripping wet.

He lay there, staring at my naked body. It was the first time any man had seen me bare, looking at every inch of me as if he had the eyes of a tiger about to eat its prey.

He slowly took off his shirt, and I saw every inch of his own toned, muscular body.

His lips again touched my neck, and chills began to creep through me. I was so engrossed by Andrei's face wanting me, the girl who only ever stood on the sidelines, that I barely heard him unbuckle his pants and tug them down.

Lying on top of me was the future Brigadier with nothing on. I'd thought about this moment for what seemed to be a lifetime but had never imagined it would happen. Why would Andrei have chosen to share a bed with me tonight?

He had so many other women to choose from, so why would he choose me? I started to get nervous, doubting myself and why he was here with me.

Andrei placed his finger on my clit and rubbed it slowly in a circular motion. My hips lifted as my middle begged for more.

By now, desire was pushing away any rational thoughts from my mind. I gave in to Andrei, and my body absorbed everything he was doing or about to do to me.

He was just beginning to insert himself into me when I pressed his chest with my hands. "Andrei, stop." I pushed him back.

"You, okay?" He looked at me, worried.

"I've never done this before," I whispered.

"You're a virgin?" He didn't seem surprised, sitting back on his haunches as if willing to give me all the time in the world to be intimate with him this first time.

"Yes," I admitted, embarrassed. I expected him to jump off me as an inexperienced girl was probably not what he wanted tonight.

Instead, he smiled. "Good girl, Cora. This pussy is mine and mine only."

He kissed me and gently entered me.

***

I'm snapped back to reality when I hear the chatter stop, and an older gentleman stands in the front of the class.

"Alright, class, it's precisely 9:00 a.m., so let's start." The man walks over to the door and begins to shut it. A black shoe in the doorway is blocking it from closing.

"Excuse me, is this Business 101?" a familiar voice asks.

"You just made it." The professor opens the door back up so that the student can enter.

"Great." The student walks in and looks around the room for an open seat before settling in directly behind me.

"Good morning, Cora," he whispers loud enough so only I can hear him. My eyes go wide.

"Andrei!" I whisper back.

Chapter Four

ANDREI

We walk up to the house, and the yard and balcony are already filled with students acting foolishly. Cans of beer and red cups occupy everyone's hands and are littered across the lawn. I look at the balcony and watch a girl keg stand as the guys around cheer her on.

"You sure you want to do this tonight?" Sasha gives me a concerned look.

We are Coalition men. Not to say we don't have our fair share of fun, but this is beyond us. While most teenage boys are doing shit like this, Sasha and I are too busy enjoying the finer things, such as a cigar and an expensive shot of vodka after a business deal. We are about money and legacies, not cheap beers and drunk sorority girls.

"We confirmed she's here tonight?" I ask him, smiling at a few girls in short dresses, glancing our way, and waving. All these girls have only one thing on their minds, which is to catch our eyes.

"Our guy said she's in there with the boyfriend," he replies nervously.

I glance at him angrily. My brow lowers. *The boyfriend.*

I only found out about Adam when I arrived in Seattle. Not once had Cora mentioned a boyfriend during winter break, and she sure didn't act like she had one that night in her room.

Sasha already thought coming here tonight was a big mistake, but I wanted to see more of what Cora has been up to here in Seattle and get to know more about her boyfriend.

Sasha and I are best friends, but he's also my second-in-command, a role he's held since we were thirteen. So, he acts on my command only, and when I make a decision, he follows it.

"Hey, guys." A tall blond guy walks over to us and reaches out to shake our hands. I'm assuming this is our Russian associate, the one Sasha knows. He's the one who told us about the party tonight and extended an invitation. He's Adam's fraternity brother but understands his loyalty to the Coalition always comes first.

I extend my hand. "Thanks for the invite tonight."

"Anything for the future Brigadier," he says, excitedly motioning us to follow him into the frat house. "Come on in, make yourself at home. My room's upstairs, if you need it for anything or anyone." As we pass the dance floor, he grins as a girl rubs her ass up against his cock.

Sasha pulls out the bottle of vodka we brought and pours us each a glass.

After a few minutes of attempting to drown out the loudness, I hear a girl's voice and follow the sound to see Cora and Adam arguing. Adam looks straight toward me. He seems upset because he's not doing anything to conceal his voice, which carries all the way to my ears.

"Do you know him?" Adam continues to look over in my direction.

"Yes. We grew up together," Cora answers with an equally loud voice as if it were a shouting contest between them. She huffs, then rolls her eyes when she sees me watching.

"In New York City? I didn't know you knew anyone from back home." He grabs her wrists.

I crack my knuckles in response, not liking other men touching what belongs to me.

"He just got here." Again, she glances in my direction. This time, her eyes avoid contact.

"Are you two close?" he asks with a snarl.

Their voices get louder, and a few students nearby glance in their direction.

"Not at all. We just grew up together. We lived in the same building." She frowns at him. She hasn't said anything to me in the past few days. She's both mad and curious as to why I'm here.

"He looks like a bad guy," he tries to warn her.

"Oh, shut up! He's just a businessman. Our fathers work together." She reaches up on her toes and kisses him. "Stop!" I hear her attempting to whisper.

He kisses her back, still looking in my direction as if doing it to spite me. Perhaps he is.

The three of us Coalition men continue to watch them.

When I found out about Cora's boyfriend, I had intended to kill him but reminded myself why I was here. If her boyfriend suddenly disappeared, she would know it was on my orders and hate us for it. Stringing him up by his ankles like a pig going to slaughter wouldn't make her admire me more, either.

So, what can I do? Now, I'm just here to be an asshole and, apparently, to make damn sure I get in their way!

I raise my bottle to him for a toast and laugh. His response is exactly what I anticipated as he fumes and storms off, leaving Cora standing there alone. After realizing people have been watching them argue, Cora takes off into the kitchen. I move my position to make sure she's still in my view.

Cora grabs a red cup and fills it with jungle juice, which the fraternity boys made. She starts to gulp quickly as she casually talks with the ladies. Her face flushes red, and her laughter volume has increased, indicating she's fast becoming drunk. But this doesn't stop her from grabbing another cup of juice and drinking it too quickly.

Cora didn't drink much when we were in high school. If someone had a party, she didn't attend. She would occasionally attend one of my parties, but only because her few female associates begged her to let them tag along.

Even then, Cora barely drank and stood to the side, watching all the foolishness. The guys would casually admire her from a distance, fearing repercussions if they got caught. The boys in New York knew we kept a close eye on her, and they wouldn't have wanted to end up tied up in the basement facing Sasha and the Savin brothers if they got too close.

The Cora I'm watching right now, drinking and dating a fraternity boy, is not the Cora we grew up with. She is trying to appear like someone else, which is why I'm here. We've given her some freedom, and she's strayed from my plan for her. She thinks she can have the best of both worlds, doesn't she? Well, I'll have to teach her she can't. It has to be our way. The Coalition way.

Adam finds her in the kitchen and kisses her. By now, he's also drunk. His mouth reaches her ear, whispering, and my blood boils to see that whatever he says makes her laugh. She's drunk enough that she's forgotten I'm watching her.

Adam grabs her hand, and she begins to walk and trips, indicating she's far too intoxicated.

Why am I standing here watching all this? This is not how a Savin man takes care of business. We don't watch from the sidelines.

"I got you, babe." Adam grips her tighter and starts to head upstairs. After a few steps, she's unable to walk, and he throws her on his shoulders.

Noticing this, Sasha stops talking to a few girls who have started hanging around us. He looks at our associate, who mouths, "Room 309." When Adam and Cora are no longer in sight, we head upstairs, too.

I stop short of Adam's room, noticing the door is closed. Carefully, I turn the knob and push it open a crack. I hear Adams' voice. "Baby, wake up."

I glance into the room and see Cora lying on what I assume is his bed.

"I am awake," Cora mumbles, unaware of what's happening before passing out.

"Baby, wake up. I want you."

Adam rubs her body with his hands, putting his face to hers and pressing his lips on her own whether she wants them or not. She doesn't react as her drunken state has her completely unaware her body is being touched. He moves his lips from hers, kissing down to her chest. He grabs her breasts with his hands, squeezing them.

His groin rubs against her body as he moans.

At this point, I'm about to kill that dirty bastard. Sasha motions for me to step aside, walking into the room. Adam, hearing someone behind him, turns around. "What are you doing in here? Get the fuck out!"

Adam, the college basketball captain, is not a tiny guy by any means. But he's no match for Sasha, who's been training for years to hurt and kill men. Sasha attacks Adam, hitting him with his fist and raining down blow upon blow. Adam grabs his assailant's head and manages to push Sasha backward. Sasha is too quick, holding Adam by the neck and getting him in a chokehold until he passes out.

When I reach the bed, I scoop Cora up into my arms.

"Andrei," she softly says. I can smell the liquor on her breath. "Where's Adam?" she wants to know.

"Soon to be dead, my love." I carry her out of the room, turning back to see Sasha reaching into the waistline of his pants, pulling out a gun, and closing the door behind us.

Chapter Five

CORA

Andrei entered me so fast that it felt like a train had just hit a concrete wall. His cock was enormous, and I wasn't ready for his forcefulness. I wasn't ready for him at all, not in any form.

I took a deep breath. "Oh my God!" Instantly, he knew he was hurting me and slowed down.

I was nervous and full of adrenaline at the same time. My body trembled. Andrei managed to calm me by kissing gently around my neck and lips, his face so close to mine, his hot breath in my ear. "I'll be slower," he said.

After his first few thrusts, it started to feel good.

I was heavily wet and helped him ease in and out of me. I listened to Andrei grunting with every movement and watched his pleasure on his face. I think the thought of being my first turned him on even more.

"You, okay?" He stopped for a second.

"Yes, I think so." I grabbed the back of his head and pulled his face in toward mine as I started to kiss him aggressively. "Andrei," I moaned.

He grabbed my legs, lifting them above my head, holding each ankle with his hands. This position made it more enjoyable as I began to moan louder.

Andrei's breathing got heavier, the harder he thrust into me. "Cora!" he yelled as he pushed further into me.

I felt the wetness around my pussy starting to drip down my thighs, oozing, forming a slow trail from me like lava escaping the mouth of a volcano. The intensity excited me, and I enjoyed having him in me, having him in my bed. I yearned for Andrei to be mine and mine only. But it was a thought that could never come true, one that was only a fantasy.

I fisted my fingers in my sheets and didn't want him to stop, but it ended when he yelled my name again, and I felt a rush of fluid inside me.

He dropped his head onto my chest and laid there for a few minutes, sweating and breathing hard. It felt like an eternity. I hugged him and enjoyed the closeness we were experiencing for the first time.

But the moment was cut short when we heard my parents walk into our condo. They must have just arrived from the Christmas Eve party. I heard a drunk laugh from my mom as they walked past my room.

Andrei quietly slipped off me. He looked down at the sheets, and my eyes followed. On my white sheets were red stains from my bleeding.

He kissed my cheek and apologized, "Sorry."

I was far too mortified to answer back. And, in minutes, he was dressed and leaving my bedroom. When I heard the apartment door close, I put my hands over my mouth and whispered to myself, "What have I done?"

***

I've dreamed of us staining my bed every night since then. "Andrei," I moan as my hand moves down my stomach and gently touches between my legs. I hear a noise but can't place it. My head is foggy from the night before. I can barely open my eyes but try to despite a splitting headache.

The ceiling and wall, in my view, are unfamiliar, instantly letting me know I'm not in my room. I breathe frantically and sit up quickly, which causes the pain in my head to pound even harder. Looking up, I see the devil I've been avoiding watching me intently.

His smug smile lets me know he was watching me as I 'almost' touched myself. *Oh gosh! Did I whisper his name aloud?*

"Where am I?"

"My room." He sits there patiently. I hate this about Coalition men. They are always so confident that they watch patiently to see you fumble and make mistakes before they attack.

"Where's Adam? How did I get here?" I try to remember last night. The last thing I recall was being in the kitchen with Adam. I may recall us walking upstairs. I slightly remember Andrei in Adam's room.

"You were drunk last night. I brought you here to watch over you." He walks over to the nightstand, handing me a water bottle.

My mouth is dry from the alcohol, and I grab his offering and gulp down the liquid, quickly regretting it when my stomach starts to turn. I begin to feel like I may puke. "I don't need you to watch me. I was fine here on my own last semester." I begin to drink the water more slowly.

"I see. You seem to be doing a good job here in Seattle, attending frat parties and getting drunk."

Andrei has moved to the bottom of the bed and sits. He's too close to me. My body can't handle him being near me as chills move down my arms and my middle tingles. But his words have annoyed me. How patronizing!

"Excuse me? What I do is none of your business." I jump out of bed, look around the floor for my shoes and spot my heels by the nightstand. I lace up the straps as fast as I can.

"Cora, everything you do is my business." Andrei grabs me. My heart starts to race.

"What do you want from me? You got what you wanted in New York, right? You wanted my first time. Well, you got that, so why do you keep bothering me?" I pull back from him and attempt to make my way out of the room.

I shove him as hard as possible to pass him, but it makes him block me more forcefully. "Andrei, move." I can't get away from him because he's tightened his grip on me.

Trapping me against the wall, I can feel the impressive bulge from his pants.

I dare to think for just a split second, that maybe, he also wants more, like I do. But it's a stupid notion. No way would he want that.

"I will not have you running around acting like a whore!" The man everyone fears rears his ugly head and growls at me. Hearing him call me a whore infuriates me. I slap him. I immediately knew I'd made a big mistake in hitting a Coalition man. But it's too late. I can't take it back.

He rubs his cheek with his hand, cocking his face to the side. I close my eyes as tears start to run down my skin.

His erection presses against me harder. My own body is a mess of emotions, lust, and anger warring within me.

"Cora, stop," I hear him whisper in my ear.

His closeness causes a spark through my thighs, my body wanting him to spread my legs and claim what's his. *What's he waiting for?*

I remind myself I'm nothing to him. Clenching my thighs, I quickly shove him to the side as I run out of his apartment.

As I stumble and trip my way through the campus, trying to find a landmark resembling something I'm aware of, my mind is muddled. I fled New York to escape the mafia and men like my father, seeking a fresh start. So why is it that the only thing I want right now is to run to Andrei, the future Brigadier and leader of the Bratva?

Chapter Six

SASHA BELOV

I'm fucking hungover with a pounding headache from a bottle of vodka last night. After our run-in with Adam, I stayed away from the apartment, giving Andrei and Cora some alone time. I can't complain. Instead, I got to spend the night with a blonde named Amy. I kept the cheerleader up all night and came on her boobs twice.

Tired and irritated, I enter the apartment to find Andrei typing at his desk.

"Did you hurt him?" he asks me.

"Not yet," I say, sounding disappointed. After Andrei left with Cora, I beat Adam up, being sure to leave him bruised all over in hidden spots. I'm trained to hurt and kill men, but I'm also trained to stay in the shadows. A dead college athlete would bring attention both to campus and to us.

I lie on the couch, hoping to nap, not worried about doing any homework for classes this week. That's because I have zero interest in getting a degree. What would I want with a better education? I already know everything that can help me in life. So, while Andrei takes the various business courses, I take the easier ones, like working out and athletic training.

Seattle appalls me. *This city sucks!* It's full of nature, and the campus reeks of coffee and granola. But it wasn't my choice. After seeing Cora this winter break, Andrei wanted to follow her here, and where he goes, so do I. I've known Andrei since we were young, and we've been inseparable since then.

From the day Andrei first gave Cora a flower in kindergarten, there was something between the two of them, even though they'd never been romantic. When another guy from our school asked her to homecoming, I made sure he was in the hospital and couldn't attend. Andrei has his mark on Cora, and she doesn't even know it.

I know Andrei was pissed when we got here and learned about Adam. To be truthful, we were both blindsided when we found out Cora had a boyfriend.

He yelled out, and he thumped his fist into a concrete wall so hard that his knuckles cracked and bled. Andrei said he had wanted to give her some space after all the fuckups he'd made in high school and with the girls he'd insisted on parading in front of her. Still, he quickly realized he had given her too much freedom.

I feel partially guilty for what happened, even now. Even though he wanted to leave her alone, I should have kept tabs on her. I won't let something big like this slip again.

Andrei is a man who gets whatever he wants. Girls chase him like his cock is dipped in melted chocolate and then encrusted in diamonds. But Cora is different. She's soft-spoken, caring, and honestly, super gorgeous for being a quiet bookworm.

Most girls born in the Coalition would kill for a chance with Andrei or any of the Savin brothers, but not her. Cora wants her own life.

"I may have messed things up today," says Andrei, who never looks up from his laptop.

"What happened?" I lie with my eyes closed, relieving some of the tension in my head.

"I was fighting with Cora and called her a whore." The crack in his voice isn't typical, and I know he regrets his harsh words.

Fuck, I think. "I'm sure that didn't go well."

Having been raised to be the future Brigadier, Andrei is usually even-tempered. Cora is the only girl who rattles him.

"She slapped me." Of course, she did. Cora is a lady who knows her worth. Andrei's met his match with her.

"Wow, you finally reached the foreplay stage with her," I say, daring to tease him, laughing. Suddenly, a book comes flying across the room, about to hit me, until I catch it.

"Fuck you!" He goes back to typing.

"Damage control?" I ask him, already knowing the answer.

"Please." His response isn't commanding. When dealing with Cora, I manage her as his friend, not his second. I guess I won't be relaxing today.

Having run into my room, I put on a clean shirt to make a good impression, then stride across the campus toward the women's hall. I walk into the building, and a group of pretty ladies look my way. Nonchalant, I walk by, giving them a smile. The women are the only things I enjoy about college.

I hastily make my way up the stairs two steps at a time to the fourth floor, then scurry down the hallway and stop at Room 403.

Knock, knock. Two confident raps with a knuckle.

Footsteps sound from inside. "Wait a minute!" she cries out. Then, shortly, Cora answers the door, looking less radiant than usual- disheveled and messy.

"What do you want, Sasha?" Her voice drifts away from me.

She hurries back to her bed and slips beneath the covers, wearing her sweats with her hair still tousled from the night before. The puffiness under her eyes reveals that she's been hiding in bed, crying.

"Heard you slapped Andrei." I close the door then look around to ensure her roommate isn't there.

"Yup. And do you know why I slapped him?" She doesn't wait for an answer. "He called me a whore!" she yells at me from under the covers. Burying her head under it signifies she doesn't want to talk to me.

I really hate getting between the two of them. "Why are we here, Cora?" I finally asked because when I asked Andrei, his only response was silence. Now, perched on the edge of her bed, I hope she'll give me an answer. "What happened when you were home on winter break that made him move across the country?"

She pulls the cover from her head and sits up, her face flushed.

"Nothing." Cora's eyes dart away from mine, and she fidgets with her fingers. She's been displaying these signs since she was little whenever she lies.

I place my hand on her leg to calm her. "Cora, you need to tell me what happened."

"Sasha, for once, can you stop being Andrei's protector? Be mine, be my protector," she screams at me, tears falling down her cheek.

"I'm trying to protect you both. I love you both!" I lean in and hug my twin sister.

Chapter Seven

CORA

Ding. My cellphone goes off again with another text message from Adam. Since the party, he's texted me fifteen times. My returned messages have been deliberately vague, telling him I haven't been feeling well.

"Dang, girl! You're going to eventually have to call him." My roommate Nicole walks over to her bed to gather her stuff.

"I know." I let out a sigh. I've spent the weekend in bed, hiding from the world, trapped in my thoughts, and snuggling under the duvet. I barely managed to squeak out a few assignments for the school week.

I wish Andrei hadn't shown up because I don't know what to do or how to handle this. I also want Adam to give me space. But Nicole disagrees.

"Adam seems like a great guy. He's a frat brother, a basketball team captain, and totally romantic. I can't imagine what he's done to make you ignore him all weekend," Nicole says, sounding like she's the one dating him. With a curious look, she waves goodbye, shakes her pretty head, and walks out the door.

I sink deeper into my pillow, the warmth of my bed so comforting that if I didn't have class, I could stay here all day and throw myself a private pity party. *Five more minutes. That's all.*

She is right, though, and I know it. Adam *is* a great guy. Last semester, when I was eager to forget New York, he was the perfect guy. But, if I have to be honest, he's never been the guy to make my stomach flutter and my pussy melt. He's not the man I think of when I'm alone. He is not the guy who makes me spread my legs and finger my clit when I'm resting in bed like this, nor is he the one who makes me orgasm so hard even thinking of him.

Andrei ... Andrei does these things.

Yes, Andrei, the boy who went from my little girl crush to the teenage boy I craved. He's always been the one, my one. Wrapped up in years of lusting over him, I was eager to give my body to him that night, wanting to believe that our lovemaking was going to feel extraordinary for both of us. A lie I now realize was always far from the truth.

Because he's just called me a whore!

I never thought he would say something so cruel to me. I've never had a man solicit such anger from me when I slapped him, either.

I had spent part of the weekend in fear, especially when Sasha came to see me. Men in Andrei's position in the Coalition have killed for less. The men would say I deserved it and not punish Andrei for my death. Not even my father would save me. Women are supposed to be loyal. Women are supposed to give in, to acquiesce, to not make life hard for men like Andrei.

Ding. Another incoming text.

I roll out of bed and head to the bathroom to get ready. I've got twenty minutes to get to class, and I still need coffee.

In the mirror, I feel taken aback by the girl staring back at me. Only a few weeks ago, a more confident Cora stood before me. Right now, I'm not so sure who I am, only that I'm a mess. I quickly throw on a dress with a pair of knee-high boots before applying light makeup.

As I run down the stairs onto the courtyard filled with students, I hear that sound again. *Ding. Ugh, Adam.* Weeks ago, the sound of a message gave me butterflies. Today, that same ding is just annoying. I'll call him tonight and deal with him. I've got business class today.

As I walk into class, I scan the room and let out a sigh of relief when I don't see Andrei. I could really use an emotional break today, but a part of me already misses him and longs for his presence.

My head is down on my keyboard when I hear a sound behind me. Without glancing up, I move my head to the right and, from the corner of my eye, see Andrei sitting in the seat behind me again.

I don't have to look back to know he's staring at me. I have felt his glares since we were kids. For a boy who made a show of hardly talking to me, he seemed to always be watching me. Not in a creepy way, but protective, making me feel safe knowing he's around.

I barely listen to the professor while watching the time on my laptop. Knowing Andrei's eyes are on me the entire class causes my cheeks to flush as heat rises from my body. I think of being in his bed that morning and that I should have let him part my knees to feel his skin against mine.

My attention snaps back to class when the professor wraps up the lesson.

I quickly gather my belongings and scurry toward the library before settling into my favorite spot, having been lucky to find this secluded area on the top floor during my first week here. It offers a quiet place to read or write, away from everyone. This corner is lined with old theses and dissertations, so no one else ever comes back here.

I settle in the corner, open my book, and enjoy a good romance novel. Today, my thoughts of Andrei have me opting for some spicy romance.

I'm completely wrapped up in my book when footsteps approach me.

"You look beautiful today." The sound of his deep voice startles me. The handsome man with hazel eyes stands behind me.

"Andrei." I put my book down and stand. My hands shake nervously.

"So, this is your new hiding spot?" He steps closer, and my back hits the wall behind me. His look is stern. I'm not sure if he's still mad at me for the slap. Andrei doesn't show his emotions. Coalition men are trained that way. Both my father and twin brother have similar mannerisms.

"How did you find me?" I didn't notice Andrei or Sasha following me earlier.

"You always hid in the quiet back corner of our high school library. Figured you'd do the same here." Heat rises in my cheeks thinking about him watching me in high school. I don't recall ever seeing him or Sasha in the library.

I lift my eyes to his face. Andrei is undeniably handsome. What I love most are his eyes.

His gaze is lustful as he traps me between himself and the wall. He rubs my lips with his thumb before grabbing my chin and placing his lips on mine. My heart starts beating frantically. When he pulls away, I lick my lips, wanting more.

"You taste delicious, Kitten," he whispers while his teeth nibble at my skin.

Kitten. That's the name he calls me when no one else is around. I've never known him to give any other girls a nickname. *Kitten* is my name, and it's mine only.

My insides begin to melt, wanting him inside of me so badly. He presses his body against me harder, letting me feel his erection against my stomach. I want to touch his cock, but I'm too nervous to make a move.

"I *may* have been out of line the other day." His comment catches me by surprise. Future Brigadiers don't apologize. Not that it is an apology, but it's halfway there. His sincerity catches me off guard, leaving me momentarily speechless. So, I stand there, casting a forgiving look.

"Let me make it up to you." He moves his hand from my face, his fingers creeping up my dress, pulling my panties to the side.

My hands try to push him away, but a moan escapes me when the tip of his finger circles my clit.

He moves his hands to each side of my panties and tugs them down my legs until he's in front of me on his knees. Seeing him kneeling below me gives me pleasure. *Did the future king just drop to his knees?* I stiffen my ass when his hand begins to move my dress past my waist. His finger quickly but intentionally gets too close to my asshole.

I look down at Andrei. Looking up at me, his eyes lock on mine as the corners of his lips twitch toward a smile. My pussy flutters in anticipation, my juices already flowing.

My self-consciousness begins to run wild. *Am I really standing here in the corner of the library with my middle exposed?* Too caught up with my thoughts, I don't take notice of Andrei's next move. Without warning, Andrei puts his face close and blows on my pussy.

Any thought of regret of how I got myself into this predicament is gone. Right now, the only thing I need is for Andrei to make me come.

Chapter Eight

ANDREI

Placing my hands on both legs, I slowly spread them as my lips kiss her inner thighs. Her skin feels cool and soft against my hands. I'm close enough to her pussy to smell her flowery scent as I suck her upper thigh, leaving a hickey only the two of us will see. Cora is mine, and I will mark her as I please.

I slowly kiss and lick around her clit, making a tiny amount of contact, teasing her. She softly moans and pushes her hips toward my mouth.

"Has anyone kissed you down here before?" My lips continue to touch her. My fingers move up and down her inner thighs, giving her goosebumps.

"No," she whimpers softly.

"Good girl, Kitten. This pussy is mine." Flattening my tongue and using my head and neck to apply pressure, I move my mouth from the base of her pussy until the tip passes over her clit. My tongue is light and barely touches her.

Cora tangles her fingers in my hair, breathing fast. I continue moving my head back and forth until her body grows tense.

"Do you want to come?" I continue licking.

"Yes." Her fingers in my hair pull me closer to her pussy. Her moans become louder as her breathing increases.

"Who owns this pussy, Kitten?" I ask her, making my kisses lighter.

"What?" She stops and looks at me.

I gaze up at her. "If you want to come, tell me the answer. Who owns this pussy, Kitten?" My tongue moves slowly and steadily up and down her wet pussy.

Her agonizing body tenses. She's on the verge of coming into my mouth. "It's yours. I belong to you," she pants.

"Say it." I continue to slow down.

"Oh my God," she manages, her words interspersed with gasps as she clutches my hair, her fingers twisting into it tighter. "This ... this pussy is ... this is ... my pussy is owned by Andrei Savin." As she comes on my face, I pick up my pace again to a steady rhythm. She tastes like heaven. I could get addicted to eating her.

She tries to pull away, and I grip her thighs steadily, not letting her move. She holds her breath, trying to calm herself.

"Breathe. Relax and enjoy my apology." I continue to lick back and forth, slowly, and steadily. She rocks her body against my mouth, and I delight in her soft whimper.

"Andrei!" escapes her lips as she comes again on my face, her waves of sensation traveling through her entire body at these full-body orgasms.

I suck her wetness, her body leaning against the wall, limp. I pull her dress back down and grab her panties. Instead of putting them back on her, I place them in my pocket, keeping them for later. Now, I gaze at the beauty standing in front of me.

There's a business meeting I am supposed to be preparing for. However, when I'd seen Cora in class, I couldn't let her get away from me, so I just had to follow her. And here I am.

She's consumed my mind all weekend, making me want to visit her. But Sasha convinced me it was best to give her a few days to settle down.

Since arriving in Seattle, I've been wrestling with my feelings. Cora is the only woman I've ever felt something for.

When I got here, what I thought was completely mine was being shared with someone else. This now causes me a pain I have never felt before and never imagined I could feel. So, knowing she's been hiding in bed crying brings me a strange feeling of contentment, assuring me that our emotional attachment is still intact.

Why did I call her a whore? Cora is far from a whore. She's saved herself for me—and me only. I knew I was wrong as soon as I said it, but apologies don't come easy. Coalition men, especially Brigadiers, don't learn to apologize. So, coming here to tell her I'm sorry is brand-new territory.

I can only hope she has forgiven me. Her pussy sure felt like it, the feeling of her shattering in my mouth divine. I've never wanted anyone so much in my life.

Thinking about it right now, there it is again, my cock strains against my pants. I'm contemplating lifting her legs around my waist before sliding into her tight pussy again. But I've still got that damn meeting to attend.

Unlike other college students, I'm the vice-president of our families' businesses in the U.S. and Russia. Of course, Dad, as President, wasted no time announcing my new role on my graduation day. I've been learning from my father my entire life, along with my brother Dmitri. I knew that taking over the vice-president role with Dmitri by my side would be an easy transition.

As his eldest son and the future Brigadier, my father has high expectations of me. It's hard enough being a businessman and a college student, so chasing a girl across the country complicates an already complicated situation. But I have to believe my Cora will be worth it, and something has been telling me that she is.

Being a Brigadier comes with some perks, which my father reminded me of when he advised me, "If you want something, you just take it." But he also knows my history with Cora and reluctantly allowed me to come.

He allowed me to come to Seattle under one condition- that I wouldn't neglect my responsibilities to our business and family.

So, my aching cock will have to wait until after I have handled these outstanding business affairs.

Her breathing is still difficult as she's still coming down from her orgasms. She shyly looks at me while her lips quirked up into a soft smile. Standing in front of me is my girl—*mine*.

I kiss her on the cheek. "See you later." I turned around to find someone watching us. For how long, I'm not sure.

"What the fuck?" Adam growls as he looks between us.

With a grin, I brush my finger against my lips to wipe Cora's wetness, licking my fingertips clean in front of him, wanting him to know I have just tasted something so delicious. Cora's taste is something I can get addicted to. Knowing I'm the only one who has ever tasted her is even more satisfying.

Adam's silence and stare tell me he's furious. But I don't care. I walk past him, bumping my shoulder against him. He pretends to be a bad guy by stiffening his shoulders like he will do something to me. For most, a tall, athletic guy is scary, but I know far scarier men. The fear they put in others isn't based on size but on how easily and mercilessly they will kill for nothing.

Before I disappear between the rows of books, I give my Kitten one last glance to find her eyeing me. She isn't even paying attention to her angry boyfriend standing in front of her, waving his arms around, and saying something I can only guess is about me.

When my eyes meet hers, she gives me a soft smile. A low laugh escapes me as I exit. *She's mine.*

Chapter Nine

CORA

I felt very vulnerable standing there, with my legs spread wide apart and Andrei on his knees in front of me with my middle in plain view. So many questions race through my mind while his face was buried in my folds. It was my first time having someone lick me there, and it felt better than good. *It was amazing!*

When Andrei's tongue first touched me, waves of pleasure surged through my body, and I wanted more of it. I grabbed his hair, pushing his face deeper into me because there was nothing, I wanted more at that moment than his mouth on me.

So wet and ticklish between my thighs, I rode what he gave me like a roller coaster. Andrei dropping to his knees in the library was unpredictable and fun. So, I did as he said and closed my eyes. I enjoyed the experience until it was impossible to hold back from exploding on his face twice. I could get addicted to that.

I become breathless, replaying the moment in my head, and my middle tingles as the wetness surges again between my legs, still without panties on. Andrei took those afterward. *Why?* I'm not sure, but it kind of turns me on thinking about him holding on to them.

Knock, knock. My thighs clench together while my mind pushes the thoughts away.

Oh my God! Adam ... Needing to rush to my writing class, I blurted out, "We need to talk about it tonight in my room. I'm not going to stand in the library arguing."

Now, that argument has arrived inescapable. "Hi." I slowly open the door.

This fight is not something I look forward to. My father always angered easily, so I shy away from arguing and fighting of all kinds, having been brought up in a world where an argument can result in physical pain and sometimes, death. That is the world I'm running from.

Adam walks into my room, hugging me into his chest. He kisses me on my forehead before saying, "I forgive you, baby."

What? He forgives me?

"I don't recall apologizing, thanks." I pull away, fully aware of owing him an apology for these past few days. Still, it's too irritating that he assumes he's getting one.

"You don't think you owe me an apology for hiding in the corner of the library with that guy?" He's starting to yell, then grabs my wrist as I try to walk away from him.

"That guy is Andrei, and I told you we grew up together. He's my brother's best friend." I shake my wrist away from him before walking to the other side of the room to give him space.

I'm frustrated by the situation, annoyed, and made uncomfortable by the hurt on his face. But at the same time, my heart breaks for him. Adam *is* a good guy, but with Andrei here, things are too complicated right now to give him what he needs.

But Adam deserves a girlfriend who loves and adores him and him alone. I have tried to be that girl, especially last semester. Adam was exactly what I was looking for when I ran away from the world I grew up in. But I can't deny that my heart has always belonged to Andrei.

When I came to Seattle, I didn't know if Andrei felt the same way toward me. And honestly, I still don't know. He's not the kind of man to yell, *I love you* from the top of his lungs. But his coming to Seattle makes me dare to feel something, allowing me to think that the feeling is reciprocated. What I feel for him, he feels in return. And I want that. I've always wanted that. More than I want Adam.

A thought flits through my head, something abhorrent but inevitable. I'm surprised Andrei and Sasha haven't hurt Adam yet. It's unlike Coalition men to let another man touch or even briefly possess what belongs to them. Andrei has called me *his* a few times. *Is he claiming me? If he is, then what is he waiting for?* It's just a matter of time before Adam gets hurt.

I have been deceiving myself, telling myself there's no harm in Adam and me and that Adam would stay safe. How could I have been so naïve?

I saw Sasha's irritation when he looked at Adam at the frat party. I know my brother. It's the look he gives before you're about to experience the 'basement,' which means you're about to acquaint yourself with the most physical pain you'll ever feel, so much so that you wish they would just kill you. *I have to do this. I have to stop this before Adam gets hurt.*

I move to the bed, patting the spot beside me.

When he sits, I grab his chin and look at him. "Adam, you are a great guy ..."

"You better not be dumping me, Cora." I hear the agitation in his tone.

I push on. "You are a great boyfriend. But, with my brother and Andrei here, it complicates things," I say as gently as possible as if that'd make the heartbreak hurt any less.

Then he pulls away dramatically. "Are you with him?"

"No. Well, maybe. We grew up together, and there's a lot of history there." Honestly, I don't know myself, so I'm not entirely lying to him. There is no right answer.

"I want you, Cora. You're mine."

Yeah, I keep hearing that a lot lately. When I hear it from one man, it makes my heart leap and sing, whereas, from the other, it makes bile rise in my throat, like right now.

"Adam. I'm sorry. I need this time to figure things out." I stand up, hearing someone outside.

He stands and stops me. "Cora, I'm not giving up on us. I love you!" I'm surprised to hear those three words, especially from him. But it doesn't change things. I don't love Adam. I can't love him because I've always loved Andrei.

As I walk toward my door, I hear a loud, hard knock. I can't have Andrei or Sasha arriving to hurt Adam. Not now, not while he's processing this.

Yet, standing in front of me is a man I fear more than both Andrei and Sasha combined.

"Dad... what are you doing here?"

Chapter Ten

CORA

My already small dorm room closes in on me as my father enters, walking past me. My arrogant father's eyes narrow on Adam. With his lips squeezed flat, he looks Adam up and down with disdain.

"Dad, what are you doing here?" I ask again nervously.

"I had work in Seattle and thought I would stop by to see Sasha." My father never once visited me last fall, sending me to college with a first-class plane ticket and two suitcases.

"Dad? Wow, it's nice to meet you, sir." Adam, shocked, reaches his hand out to my father.

"Who are you?" my dad snarls, gritting his teeth, never removing his hands from behind his back.

Adam quickly retracts his hand, and it's clear in the moment that this isn't what he imagined when first meeting my dad. "I'm Adam, Cora's boyfriend," he attempts, his voice shaking.

My father's gaze darts to me, and his face tenses. "You can't be. Cora isn't allowed to have a boyfriend." My breathing accelerates, adrenaline rushing through my body. My father is upset by Adam being in his presence, believing anyone not in the Coalition must be inferior.

Adam stands there, uncertain of his next move. He confessed his love for me and seemed enthusiastic about meeting my father, but now he knows he's made a grievous mistake.

My father is not a kind man. He grew up in the Coalition and lives for the Bratva, nothing more. He has no love for me either, finding me just an inconvenient 'thing' that came along with his pride and joy, Sasha.

"Adam, I think it's time for you to go. I'm sure you have a practice you need to get to," I say with a faint smile. Opening the door, I find myself gesturing for him to leave.

With one last glance at my father, Adam nods before exiting. Turning back at me, he stares with pity. Embarrassed, I shut the door on him.

A tear runs down my cheek because now, I am alone with my father again, and punishment is inevitable.

I slowly turn around to feel a sharp blow sting my face as my body slumps against the wall. Holding pressure to my cheek, I begin to whimper.

A hand brushes against my scalp as he fists my hair, pulling me further into the room and throwing me onto my bed. I lie in the fetal position, crying, crossing my arms around my body in anticipation, the certain expectation of more hits.

Grabbing my chin forcefully to make our eyes meet, he bares his teeth, growling, "You slut! Did you sleep with that boy? You disgust me."

"No, Dad," my faint voice answers.

He stares me in the eyes, his pupils cold as ice.

"Don't lie to me!" His rage sears through his tone, unmistakable. He pushes me further into the bed, the pressure sending an unrelenting pain through my lower back. When he lets go of me, all I see is a monstrous figure towering over me, a shadow that blocks out all reason.

My father cracks his knuckles, and this is just the beginning. I remember every hit and every curse word he's called me. It started when I was a little girl.

***

"What did you do?" Sasha grabbed my hand and pulled me into the corner.

"I didn't do anything." I began to cry as I leaned into his chest.

"Then why is Father upset?" He peeped around the corner.

"I don't know. He came home from work and yelled at me."

My brother looked at me bravely, but the fear shone in his eyes. "What did he say?"

"That 'this' is my fault. That his business is in ruins because the Savin family wants me."

"Why would they 'want' you?" We both looked at each other, baffled.

As we looked up, a specter crept to our side, and our father stood in front of us.

"Sasha, it's time for you to go do your homework." Father put his hand on Sasha's shoulder, assuring him everything would be okay. For him, it would be.

"And Cora?" Sasha paused.

A manic laugh sent shivers down my spine. "Cora needs to be punished."

Before me, my father turned into a monster.

Around the time I was ten, my father started 'punishing' me.

He had always been mean to me but mostly ignored my existence. However, something after that made him more interested in me and more protective, to the point he started hitting me if he thought I was getting out of line.

I don't know what changed that day. The only thing I know for certain is that one day, after a business meeting with the Savin family, he came thundering into my room and raised his hand high, beating me, blaming me for his business being in ruin.

After that, he took it out on me whenever he was disgruntled with Mr. Savin or if I did anything to make him question my virtue.

I was a little girl when he started doing it, not even aware of what kind of business my father ran. At that time, I didn't even know about the Bratva either, only that my dad seemed different from the other dads I saw at school.

I grew up in a world rife with secrets, crime, and violence. The men looked like businessmen with expensive suits and gold watches, but I didn't ever see the other dads with armed security and guns in their hands. These men live by an oath, and the Coalition is always set to be the most important thing, even more than their wives and children.

We grew up with the Savin family. Our fathers worked together, although Mr. Savin was higher ranked and one of the leaders of the Coalition.

As for Sasha and me, we had known the Savin brothers our entire lives, so he and the brothers were friends. But Andrei and his brothers barely acknowledged me except when our families were together. After Andrei gave me flowers in kindergarten as an apology for pulling my hair and making me cry, his younger brother, Dmitri, would tease him about me.

"Andrei! Is she your girlfriend?" he'd taunt, and that would make my face pink and make Andrei cringe and shrug, squirming in his equally embarrassed skin.

Eventually, Andrei would look at me and tell his brother to shut up. And I still have those flowers, even to this day.

As for Mrs. Savin, she has always shown me kindness, even when I was a little girl.

She and my mother grew up in the Coalition together and were firm friends. I would accompany my mother and sit in the corner at their luncheons, reading my books and staying out of their way, content to be silent and alone.

But sweet Mrs. Savin would talk to me, asking me about what I was reading while combing her fingers through my hair, often commenting on how beautiful I was. One day, she looked at me and straightened my hair, removing it from my eyes and gently tucking the strays behind my ears before she told me

I would make a great wife when I grew up. I recall smiling and shrugging, telling her maybe after I went to college and became an author.

She pressed her lips together and replied, "Dear, you never know what the future holds for you." She kissed me on the forehead, making me feel special.

***

Another strike sharply hits my face as I scream, "Dad, please!" I fall onto the floor and crawl to the corner of my room to cower under the desk like a beaten dog.

"You think Andrei wants a slut for a woman?" He raises his hand in the air, ready to strike me again.

"Dad. I didn't do anything with Adam. I promise. Please," I plead with my arms crossed in front of my face, trying to protect myself the only way I can. But with an open palm, he hits me again.

"What would Andrei say if he was here?" The redness in his face is evident in his tone. He moves to strike me again, but a clicking sound echoes from behind my father, drawing my gaze past him to see the gun barrel.

Behind my father is Andrei, holding a gun to the back of my father's head.

"He would say, 'Don't fucking touch her again.'"

Chapter Eleven

ANDREI

"What the fuck, Sasha?" I shove my friend against the wall. "You knew about this?"

"It's family business." He shoves me back, though neither of us pushes hard despite the anger. It would be too easy for our tempers to get out of control.

"Cora is my business." My fist hits his shoulder.

I slow down and focus on my breathing, pacing around our apartment. "How long has he been hitting her?" My voice lowers so Cora doesn't hear us.

"Since we were kids, I guess." He leans against the wall, arms crossed.

"But he doesn't hit you?" I lean in toward him, eyeing him intently for any lies.

"No, never," he asserts, his voice full of guilt.

I walk over to the bar and grab a glass of vodka. Sasha follows me and grabs another one.

"Look, I think it has something to do with your family." With curiosity, Sasha looks up from his glass at me.

"The Savins?" I'm perplexed.

"When we were little, he never hit her. But, one day, he came home blaming her for ruining his business and yelling about your family. That's when he started hitting her."

I know exactly what day he's referring to. It's my secret. A secret I'm not ready to share with Cora yet.

"Why didn't you tell me?" I feel guilty for not knowing and not protecting her before.

"Why would I?" he screams at me.

"Because she's mine," I tell him possessively, gritting my teeth in anger.

"Really?" He slams his glass down. "You didn't care about Cora when your cock was deep inside all those other girls when you were growing up, did you? You didn't care about her when we were fucking the same girls, sometimes balls deep in them together. Cora wasn't yours then. So, now you want to claim my twin sister?"

"Things are different now," I say with a loud but exasperated sigh, then take a big gulp of vodka.

"Why? What happened during winter break that we suddenly moved across the country to Seattle?" He stares at me.

Because of guilt, I didn't share what happened over winter break with Sasha. I look away, still feeling guilty.

"Motherfucker! You fucked my sister!" he cries, slamming his fist against the wall. "I told you to stay away from her."

"And I told you, I can't."

"For fuck's sake. What is the deal with you and my sister? Why is your family so interested in her?" I see the hand on his side clench into a fist.

"Your mom adores her. It's not just you. Your father and brothers also watch her all the time." He throws his glass in the sink before picking up his jacket.

"Why didn't you protect her?" I yell at him. "She is your sister. Not only that ... your twin."

Marching across the room, he pauses before he leaves. Looking back at me, he whispers, "Because it would have made it worse." The door slams before I can say more.

I gulp down the remaining vodka before making my way to my bedroom. There, I find a wet Cora wrapped in a towel, stepping out of my bathroom.

"Are you and my brother arguing?" Her voice is still shaky from the events of tonight.

"Just guy stuff," I reply, grabbing a shirt from my drawer.

"I hope it's not about me, that's all." She lets out a soft cry. Her towel falls to the floor as she puts on the shirt. I immediately advert my gaze because she's self-conscious.

My eyes wander when she looks away, and her hardened nipples are enough to make my cock strain against my pants.

"Just business. Nothing for you to worry about." Noticing a dark circle around her cheek, I gently touch it.

"Make-up will cover it tomorrow," she says as if it is nothing.

She turns her gaze away, and I can almost see the shame etched on her face, which fills me with sadness. She shouldn't feel ashamed of her father's actions; it's not her fault- it's entirely on him, as he's the real monster. I am the one guilty of not knowing about it and failing to protect her all these years.

"Look at me," my voice commands her. Then I grab her chin so that our eyes meet. "He will never hurt you again." She moves her head away, but I hold her harder. "I promise. You're mine, and no one touches what belongs to me."

Her eyes soften, a tear falling onto her cheek and making its way down.

I lean down and touch her lips with mine, a kiss filled with emotions—guilt, affection, and desire—all simultaneously.

My gaze drops to her body, to her thin frame drowning in my shirt, but the thought of what's underneath has my cock aching for her. She must feel my bulge pressing up against her because she is pressing her thighs together. I smirk as she bites her lower lip, unable to control myself.

I slip my shirt over my head and watch her do the same, pulling her close and kissing her neck as my hands loosen my belt. After my pants hit the floor, I lift her to the bed and gently lay her on her back. I place myself between her open thighs, softly kissing her body. Cora's lips curl upward, and she giggles, flipping us over until a sexy Cora sits on top of me.

My hands gently touch her thighs, causing her hips to move against my cock. She moans softly when I grab hold of it myself and place it right there at the entrance to her tight pussy. She takes the full length into herself, then moves in sync with me as she rides me. She's in control, choosing the pace and depth as her pussy rides my cock.

Watching her try to dominate me makes me harder in her, so hard I almost don't believe it's possible.

With each hand on her rounded breast, I flick her nipples with my fingers. Her moans get louder as her thighs move up and down, thrusting deeper. Moving my hand down her stomach, touching her lightly, my finger stops at her clit. I rub it in a circular motion.

"Andrei!" she cries.

"Ready to come?" I watch her as her body starts to move faster.

"Yes!" She places her hands on my chest, riding me harder.

"Not yet." I hold her thighs tight against me, thrusting my waist up, shoving my cock deeper into her pussy.

"You ready?" I ask her, watching her face as she's on edge, trying to hold on to her orgasm.

"Yes, please!" Her moans turn into screams.

"Come for me, Kitten." When her wetness soaks my cock, I fill her with my juices as her body shakes. Her cum mixes with mine and starts to seep from her pussy. I leave my cock in her as her body lies on me.

"Andrei," she whispers.

I wrap my arms around her, pulling her tightly against my chest. "Was that better than the first time?"

"Fuck, yes!" She laughs, closing her eyes.

"Go to sleep. You're safe with me, Cora," I promise her. She lets out a sigh, relaxing her body. Within minutes, a soft whistle escapes her.

I continue to hold her for hours, my eyes wide open. Rage burns inside of me, lying here, thinking- *Mr. Belov will pay for hurting her!*

Chapter Twelve

SASHA

I stood up, yelling, "Yea, touchdown!" Andrei jumped up next to me, and we gave each other high-fives. New York just scored seven points to secure the win.

"It's not like they won the Championship. Calm down!" Dmitri Savin remained seated.

"You don't understand. Every touchdown is a win," I yelled, excitedly grabbing the football and tossed it to Andrei, who ran across the room to catch it. We both jumped up and down, hands in the air. "Touchdown!" we both yelled. Dmitri rolled his eyes.

I spent most of my Sundays growing up at the Savin condo, watching the game. With only Cora at home, it was far more enjoyable to watch football with the guys than with her. Cora would only sit next to me, reading her book as if nothing was happening.

"Wouldn't that be cool if we played football in college, Andrei?" The thought of me playing in a big stadium with thousands of fans watching me was exciting.

Andrei sat back on the couch. He was acting weird that day as if something really bothered him. "Maybe in another life. I'll be busy in college working on becoming Brigadier."

I felt sorry for him sometimes. Being Brigadier was a high honor in the Coalition, but it came with a lot of responsibility.

The Pakhan sits at the head of the Coalition ruling the Bratva, with five Brigadiers and five families running the Bratva operations under him. Andrei's father is a Brigadier, and his grandfather was too, so the position runs in the family. In fact, you could say that becoming Brigadier was Andrei's birthright. He had been raised to become a future leader in the Coalition.

And, of course, because of becoming a Brigadier, Andrei would become one of the most powerful men in the underground world. But it also meant he had to live the life his father had planned for him, a future ordained for him long ago. Andrei would run the Savin empire one day, rumored to be worth over a billion dollars.

While most teenage boys enjoyed video games and hanging out with friends, Andrei and his brother Dmitri could do no such things, often attending business meetings with their father instead. School vacations were spent in their father's office or in the field, training with weapons. Becoming Brigadier and truly earning that status was something Andrei had to work for— seemingly, all the time.

So, my friendship with Andrei was special to him, and I knew that. We played football together on the school's field and watched New York football every Sunday during football season. It was 'our' thing. I always thought Mr. Savin was nice to let Andrei have Sundays off to watch the games with me. It was a day we both looked forward to every week.

"It's okay. You can come to my games when you're not in class."

We looked at each other, laughing. Even Dmitri joined us and chuckled. I sucked at playing football, but it didn't stop me from enjoying the game.

"What do you think you're going to do when we graduate?" he asked.

"I don't know. Guess I'll probably follow you to college. What else am I going to do? Plus, college girls are hot," I responded truthfully, having never considered my future before.

"Well, if you're going to go to college with me, then maybe we should make it official?"

"How so?" I sat up, curious.

"Are you interested in becoming my second-in-command?" He looked over at me.

"You're joking, right?" My body tingled with excitement.

"No. I think I should choose someone I can trust. Someone I consider my brother, even if we're not blood." He was serious.

Dmitri nodded in agreement.

"Andrei, my loyalty will always be to you. Hell, yes!" I jumped up from the couch, no longer paying attention to the game I'd been so eager to watch just moments ago.

"Then it's official. Welcome to the Savin family, Sasha." He reached out his hand.

I quickly shook it but suddenly realized I didn't know exactly what my job was, "We're thirteen. What am I supposed to do as your second-in-command?"

"Start learning how to shoot a gun." It was his first command as he pointed in the direction of Nikolai's room.

The game had just ended, and our team had won by a field goal.

"Well, the game's over. Guess I'll start training then." I headed to Nikolai's room to talk about my training regime. At eight, he had already murdered his first victim. We didn't know then that thousands more men would be drowning in crimson by his hands.

I looked back at Andrei, asking, "Anything else?"

"Yes. Your number one priority is to protect Cora." His eyes told me that he meant it.

"My sister? I can do that!"

***

That was seven years ago. It was a promise I took to heart. But I hadn't protected her, had I? Not from our father. It was too late for that.

Security steps aside as I enter the room. "Sasha." With a welcoming voice, a tall, thin man stands from his chair to hug me.

"Dad," I try to remain calm. After our awkward embrace, I sit next to him.

"What brings you by?" He sits with his legs and arms crossed.

"What are you doing in Seattle?" I ask him.

"I had business to attend to. Figured I'd see you while I'm here." His response falls flat, and I know whatever has brought him here is not good.

I scratch my forehead with my finger and warn him, "Dad, Andrei is pissed."

"Fuck Andrei!" He smirks, lighting up his cigar. "Why would I care about Andrei?"

"Dad, we don't need to make enemies with the Savin family," I plead with him, walking over to the bar to pour a glass of vodka.

"The Savin family. They think they're so fucking important because they're Brigadiers. They bleed like any other man," he says, talking over me.

I gulp the drink and pour another one before sitting back down. "Don't say that."

His arrogance is annoying.

"Son, it's time for you to stop playing with that Savin boy. Come home and join me in running the family business." He puffs a cloud of smoke in my face.

"That Savin boy is a future Brigadier, Father. He's appointed me his second-in-command," I remind him.

"Don't settle for being his helper. Become a boss. The Savins don't know what's coming to them." He smirks, looking at me with disappointment.

"What the fuck does that mean?" I ask. The Savins have treated me like family, and don't deserve any bullshit from my father.

He leans further back into his chair and silently smokes his cigar.

After downing a second glass of vodka, I turn to him. "And, what about Cora?"

His eyes dart to me, and with disgust, he asks, "What about her?"

"Why keep punishing her for something the Savin family did?" This is a question to which I've wanted an answer since we were ten.

"Because your sister's a slut. That's all you need to know." My face tenses, detesting how my father speaks negatively about Cora.

"Do you even know her? She's never even been with a man until Andrei. She loves him."

His laughter fills the room. "So, that slut finally fucked Andrei?" he spits, then laughs again.

Quickly standing up, I grab my gun that's tucked in the back of my pants and hold it next to me with a warning. "Stop calling her that!"

I see movement around the room, three security guards now having their guns pointed at me.

My father stands. "You've forgotten what family you belong to, boy. You're a Belov, not a Savin. You might want to remember that."

"Cora is a Belov as well. Maybe 'you' should remember that." I grit my teeth and press my finger on the trigger, ready to shoot if a bullet heads my way. He might be my father, but I'm not stupid enough to think he won't kill me.

"Son, she hasn't been a Belov in a long time." He pats my shoulder, walking past me.

"Dad." Confused by his statement, I know there's more to this story.

"The Savin family thinks their power and money makes them untouchable. It's time for new blood at the head of the table." His words fade as he walks away, leaving me standing there. He retreats into the bedroom and shuts the door, signaling that he wants to end this conversation.

It doesn't take long to understand why my father is visiting. He's starting a war, and I need to decide where my loyalties lie.

Chapter Thirteen

CORA

I tap my knuckles against the door loudly.

"Come in," Professor Cullen calls out as I twist the doorknob.

"You wanted to see me?" He waves his hand toward the chair as I sit.

Looking through the stacks of paper, he pulls out my recent assignment. After looking at it for a few minutes and rifling through his notes, he exhales heavily, taps a finger on my paper, then says, "I was very disappointed by your recent assignment."

Taking off his glasses, he leans back in his chair. "I normally don't get involved in my students' affairs, but is something going on at home?"

"No, why would you ask?" I'm surprised by his question.

"Cora, this is an advanced writing class, and you must submit a story to get in. I read your work. You're a great writer, but this story you submitted isn't good."

He returns my assignment with annotated notes scribbled throughout. The pages are filled with comments about the lack of passion between the love interests, a dull plot, and insufficient world-building to flesh out the protagonists' lives. After reviewing his feedback, I can't help but agree- *my paper is shit.*

"Maybe I've just been slightly stressed with all my classes. I know I can do better than this." For the first time, I'm admitting to myself that Andrei's presence is impacting my work and not in a positive way. I need to remind myself that I came to Seattle to escape the mafia, and for those few months last semester, I tasted freedom. But now, Andrei's arrival has dragged back all the burdens of being a Coalition child.

"Look, it's only one assignment. You will have plenty of opportunities to get your grade up. You're a great writer, and I do believe you have the potential to become a brilliant author."

Relief washes over me because Dr. Cullen is known for being a great mentor to his students. That's why I worked so hard to get into his class. Disappointing him again is not an option.

"Thank you."

"What are your plans for the summer?" he asks and begins to type on his computer.

"I'm not sure." I haven't even thought about it.

"There is an opportunity for students to take writing classes over the summer. The best part is that it's in London."

"That would be a great way to spend my summer!" I am enthused, happy to see his eyes crinkle with approval as a broad smile graces his face.

"Wonderful. The application is due in a few weeks, and you must submit a writing piece. If you want, I would be happy to provide feedback on your writing before you submit it."

I stand up, gripped by excitement. "Absolutely, Dr. Cullen. I am going to work so hard on this. Thank you for the opportunity."

After meeting with my professor, I head to the coffee shop, where I find a table in the back corner and grab a seat that gives a clear view of the front door, a habit of my upbringing.

When Adam walks in, the other female students recognize him and say hi, again clamoring for his attention. He casually waves at them before heading in my direction.

Sasha checked in with me last night and notified me they were traveling to New York for the day because Andrei had a meeting with his father. When you're in the Savin family, having a private jet to travel across the country for a one-day meeting is a nice privilege he and Sasha get to enjoy.

After a quick hug, we sit and order coffee.

"Hi." I give him a polite smile.

"Hey, beautiful." He smiles back at me with his cute dimples.

"Adam, I'm sorry…" He reaches across the table, placing his hand on mine. I politely remove it, knowing if Andrei saw him touching me, he would disapprove.

"It's okay, Cora." Our coffees arrive as an awkward moment passes. "After meeting your dad, I understand why you need space."

"Thank you, Adam, for being a good first boyfriend."

"What? I was your first boyfriend?" he chuckles.

"Um, yes. And a good boyfriend you were," I say, admitting that Adam had been precisely what I needed then, but things have changed.

"I'd assumed, with all the history between you and your brother's friend, he must have been your first." I blush. He may not have been the first to hold the boyfriend title, but Andrei is indeed my first. My first love. My first fuck. My first everything.

"I wasn't lying when I said you're a great guy, and any girl will be happy to have you. Friends?" I ask him sincerely as I do care for Adam, just not in a romantic way.

"Absolutely!" he agrees.

The door creaks open, and out of habit, I quickly look at it and find Nicole coming through the doorway. I wave at her to catch her attention. She immediately looks at us with widened eyes.

"Are we getting back together?" she asks curiously.

"Just two friends having coffee," Adam replies, annoyed.

With a side-eye, she ignores him and tells me she's just buying a cup of coffee before her study group. We exchange our goodbyes and with coffee in hand, she heads out.

We sit for hours, catching up on classes and gossiping. He offers me the motivation and support I need when I share the news about my bad grade and the opportunity this summer. He seems thrilled at my chance to visit London. It's nice to have someone to talk to and laugh with. I will miss this.

I look outside, finding the sun's already set. "Guess I should head out."

"It's dark and not safe. Let me walk you to your dorm," Adam offers.

"Thank you, but I've got stops to make. I'll see you around."

Adam and I hug before leaving, the kind of fleeting embrace of two strangers just being polite. He looks sad now, though, in a way, he must be relieved to know where he stands with me.

Seattle is cold and dark this time of year, and the university's streetlights offer a little source of light as the trees create many dark spots along my walk.

When the noise of scuffles is heard behind me, I glance back. A few other students are walking the same path, listening to music, or engaged in conversation. Deciding to cut across one of the quadrants, I leave the street, cutting through a pathway where several historical and modern buildings fill both sides of the walkway. Still, this area has no dorms, so it's a lonely walk.

Yet I am not alone, light footsteps audible behind me. Quickly turning, I find nothing but darkness and stillness, the same shadows the darkness always brings. *Nothing to panic about,* my mind tells me.

By now, it is cold enough to see the breaths escaping my lips.

I pull my jacket tighter and continue walking, soon hearing those footsteps again. My pace quickens, but so does the other set of steps. Suddenly, a sense of aloneness grips me. This is somehow terrifying, despite the walk's familiarity to me.

Another few blocks, and I'll be on the main street. I stop and look behind. Nothing. It's too dark, and the trees make the walkway darker! That's what scared me. Just my imagination.

Yet it is not. My heart stops upon noticing a dark figure loitering under a tree not too far away, but that's all I can see in the darkness.

I turn around again, beginning to jog the rest of the way. But that eerie presence is getting closer, and my jog becomes a flat-out run. Around the corner, I find myself on the main street again, heart pounding, my mouth dry. But at last, there is my dorm building. The street is busy and filled with many students heading from the dorms to the dining facilities.

As I enter my building, I look back in the direction of the walkway, seeing the shape unmistakable there, still languishing, and see a man standing there looking back at me. The darkness covers his image, and his hat covers his face, so I cannot identify him.

Once in the building, there is an immediate relief in being surrounded by students. After responding to a few hellos, I run up the stairs two at a time, scurrying to my room. It's not until I unlock my door and apply the deadbolt that I can breathe.

Safe again.

When I turn around, I find three men are standing near my bed, waiting for me.

Chapter Fourteen

ANDREI

"Andrei!" Cora screams, running into my open arms.

I kiss her beautiful lips and rub her cold cheeks with my finger, then pull her closer into a warm hug.

"What's wrong?" Sasha cuts off our moment.

"What?" Cora pulls away from me.

"What's wrong?" Sasha asks again, this time more forcefully.

"Nothing." Her head shakes, then she turns her back to us, taking off her jacket and throwing it across her bed.

"You're lying." As her twin, Sasha has always been able to tell when she isn't being truthful. I envy the fact that he knows every small thing there is to know about his sister.

"I thought I saw someone," she ventures at last, her voice quivering.

He's right. Something is wrong. I thought her pale face was due to the cold, but she's scared. "What? Who?" I signal for her to sit on her bed, unsurprised that our enemy would watch her.

"I don't know, couldn't see him. It was too dark."

Placing her fingers in mine, I hold her hand to comfort her.

"We need to talk," Sasha says with a concerned look, then moves to the other side of her.

"Did I do something?" She sounds guilty. Which she is but I'll punish her when we're alone.

I pull a strand of her hair and place it around the back of her ear. "The only thing you did is make me miss you." I lick her lips with my tongue before forcing it down her throat. My cock has been throbbing since the plane ride home, thinking of seeing Cora tonight.

"Sitting here!" Sasha reminds us, annoyed.

I give him a grin. When I'm with Cora, I get so caught up in how beautiful she is, liable to easily forget everything around me.

"Glad you two are finally together, but I don't need to see it."

A small cough escapes the guy standing in the corner. I glance up to see an old buddy from high school. "Cora, this is Michael."

"Hi." She frowns. Her eyes linger on the wide shouldered guy, wondering why he's in her room.

"He's your new bodyguard," I regret telling her, already knowing she's going to be pissed.

"Andrei, no!" Furious, she stands, crossing the room as if to flee from Michael. "I came here to get away from security and all this. I can't go to class with a bodyguard attached to me."

"Cora, it's for your protection," I growl.

"I said no," she yells.

"This is not up for discussion. I've given my order." But I say it as though she listens to me like my men do.

Sure enough, she reminds me I'll never be able to boss her around. "I'm not one of your men. I don't have to listen to you." Then she positions herself for a standoff. All I can do is stand to meet her stance.

"Cora, someone is making moves against my family," I elucidate. "It's someone close, Cora, and you know what that means for you. They'll know how much you mean to me."

She visibly bristles. "I know how to look after myself," she says.

I grip her upper arms, making her face up to me and this situation. "Look, there's only one way to say this. That guy following you is not a coincidence," I warn her.

"Maybe." She looks defiant.

Grabbing her chin, I look into her eyes. "For the final time, I told you, you're mine. I will not let anything happen to you. But, to protect you, Michael is going to be around."

"Fine, but I don't like it," she huffs, dropping her shoulders in eventual defeat.

"Cora, being with a Brigadier means security all the time. You know our life."

I order Michael to be outside her door at eight o'clock, ready to accompany her to class.

I shut the door on the men and turn to see her licking her lips. "What time will your roommate be back?"

Smiling, Cora replies, "Not until morning."

Standing in the middle of the room, I call her, "Come here, Kitten."

She slowly moves closer to me, her eyes full of flames from her desire. I stare at her, making her anxiously wait, carefully detaching and removing my cufflinks.

"Did you miss me?" I ask.

She bites her lower lip and nods.

"Show me, Kitten. How much did you miss me?"

Cora drops to her knees in front of me. Without hesitation, Cora quickly unbuckles my belt and unzips my pants. Roughly pulling them down, she licks my tip, circling it with her tongue. Slowly sucking and licking on it from top to bottom as if it's a massive lollipop, her tongue relentlessly teases my head.

"I don't know if all that will fit in my little mouth," she says, slightly embarrassed as she looks at my cock as if I'm expecting her to eat it whole. Well, maybe I am.

"I'll help you. Relax your jaw." I pull her jaw open with my finger.

She exhales and relaxes her mouth as she takes my cock all at once, now making it look so easy.

It feels amazing!

Placing my hand on her head, I shove my cock further down her throat and she continues to deepthroat me, appearing happy in her task. The sounds from her sucks and licks make me want to come fast. Without warning, my fluids spill into her mouth but she continues to suck me dry without hesitation or pause. She drinks every last drop, her big eyes fixating on mine.

"Stand up," I order her. She complies, wiping the corner of her mouth on the back of her hand.

"Take your clothes off." As she commences quickly taking off her jeans, I give a second command. "Slow. I want to watch."

She unstraps her bra and throws it across the room before covering her tits with her arms.

Holding up my pointer finger, I shake it to say 'no.' No way do I want those tits to be hidden away from me.

Dropping her arms, my cock is hard again from seeing her hardened nipples.

"Turn around. Bend down while taking off your panties." With her ass in my view, she firmly places her two fingers and slides her lace down her legs.

I move myself forward, sliding up against her ass, rubbing it. *She has a great ass.*

Next, I kiss her neck and nibble on her ear before whispering, "Bend over and put your hands on your bed." Right after she does, I slap her ass cheeks.

"Andrei!" she gasps.

"Don't move. Cora, have you been a bad girl today?" I ask, smacking her ass again.

Her ass cheeks tighten as she screams, "No! I am always a good girl!"

"You wouldn't be lying to me, would you?" One more smack. I will punish her until her ass is red as fire. That's how I feel right now, firing red because my girl was spending time with an ex today, and I know it. She is lying to me, but it provides the reason for giving this delicious punishment.

"Andrei!"

"Did I give you permission to have coffee with Adam today?" Her body tightens as she knows what's coming.

"You were spying on me?" She yelps when my palm contacts her ass again.

"Cora, do you think I would let my girl run around campus unprotected?"

"I felt bad for him. I just wanted to apologize," she pleads.

"And you think I care about that asshole?" Then, I slowly place my cock in her. "Now make me forgive you. Beg for it." Now I'm pleading with her, thrusting into her needy pussy.

Her hips rotate as she rides my cock. "Good girl, Kitten." Holding her hips, I thrust my cock into her deeper. The louder she moans, the harder I thrust.

Cora's tight pussy around my cock makes me orgasm so intensely that it spreads through my whole body and goes on for what seems like a full minute.

Not being a greedy bastard, I flip Cora over and lay her on the bed. "Relax." My fingers play with her perfect pussy until she writhes and squirms against them, then finally comes on my fingertips, unable to hold back. Holding my fingers to her lips, she licks her own juices, completely spent.

Lying by her side, I run my fingers through her hair. Being close to Cora fills my heart. I've longed to stay in bed with her at night since I was a little boy. This moment right here is what I want to fight for every day.

"How did you know I went to the coffee shop?" Her voice is weak from her loud moans.

"Michael was watching you today," I answer honestly.

"Then where was Michael when that man was following me?"

"Michael left you with Adam and came to meet me. A mistake he will pay for tomorrow." I ordered him not to leave her side. He disobeyed those orders.

"Should I be scared?" her cracked voice asks.

"No. It would be best if you didn't worry. Concentrate on your studies. Sasha and I will take care of the situation."

She digs her head further into my chest and closes her eyes.

When I find the man who scared Cora tonight, he will pay with his life. That's the Coalition way.

Chapter Fifteen

SASHA

A war is starting, but men are always fighting in our world. The only thing that ever changes is which enemy we're shooting at.

Not many men have balls big enough to go after the Savin family. Whoever we're at war with must be powerful or stupid. I play my dad's words over in my head, but I don't think it's him. Dad has hated Mr. Savin for years. The Coalition is all about rank, and my dad doesn't have it.

I know there's a story behind my dad's hatred for the Savins, their interest in Cora, and the secret Andrei keeps. I also know they're all connected. But as Andrei's second-in-command, my role is to follow orders, not to question the boss when it's clear he's not ready to share. One day, though, the truth will come to light. But honestly, it doesn't matter. Whatever Andrei does, I have his back.

Hidden, I watch Andrei and Cora have their first official date as a couple. He knew it would mean a lot to her, so I know he's put great effort into it. They look so much in love and happy together.

I don't know if I'll ever have someone in my life who steals my heart the way my twin sister steals away Andrei's, so obvious to anyone who sees them. And maybe it's best if I don't ever have anyone like that so I can stay committed to the Coalition. Seeing them together makes me happy and that's good enough for me for right now.

Michael sits at a table nearby, guarding Andrei while I watch from a distance. If someone is watching Cora, I want to find out who he is. I look along the street. It's dark, so it's hard to see shadows. For the last hour, I've been patiently standing in this fire staircase.

Students and professors line the streets, making it difficult to find someone acting suspiciously among the crowds. But I do soon notice a guy standing outside the bookstore, pretending to read his book. His eyes wander toward the restaurant more than they look at the text, and I swear he hasn't flipped a single page since standing there.

I text Andrei. *I think I see him.*

I'll see you after dinner, he replies.

After whispering something to Michael, Andrei continues his dinner with Cora as though he has no care in the world beyond the beautiful girl across from him.

I dash down the stairs until I reach the street. I duck into the coffee shop and grab a black coffee, my eyes never leaving the man who's loitering nearby.

If he knows Andrei and Cora, he knows who I am too, so I need to stay hidden. Waiting for Michael to quietly unlock the car and slide into the driver's seat, I approach the guy from behind until I'm close enough to press my gun against his flesh. "Get in the car."

"I'm just reading," he replies. "What's your problem?"

What is my problem? I think. *You'll soon see what my problem is.*

"I won't repeat myself. I have no issue leaving a dead man on the street." I unclip the safety.

Closing his book and tossing it in the trash, he follows my lead until we both slide into the car's back seat. I signal Michael to drive, though my gun never stops pointing at the stranger.

Once we're at the warehouse, Michael ties him up, my handgun pointed at his head the entire time, so he doesn't fight back.

"Who are you?" I ask the young kid who looks around our age. Not old enough to be anyone of importance. If he were a legacy child, we would already know him, being legacy kids ourselves. Legacy children are sons and daughters of organized crime leaders. We grow up together, friends or enemies, and perhaps one day, we kill each other.

His stone-cold expression reveals nothing. After a few moments of staring at him, I notice his facade crack as he starts to laugh. The first sign of a nervous man under pressure. He's inexperienced in this life.

Well, I know just the thing to introduce him to men of the Coalition. I walk over to the black bag I grabbed from the trunk and pull out the first thing placed on the top. I walk over to him, wielding the hammer in my hand and hit him on his kneecap. He yells in pain. I plan to make him scream all night if I must. I whack his other knee.

"He isn't Russian." Andrei walks in behind me.

"Obviously," I reply, standing in front of the Jamaican kid with dreads, the one who's crying.

"Again, who are you?" Andrei asks.

I hold up the hammer to hit him again.

"Ajani!" he screams.

Andrei and I look at each other confused. We have no dealings with Jamaicans, so why would they go after Cora? I ask him, "Why are you following my sister?"

"Who's your sister?" When the kid gives me a confused look, I connect my knuckle to his jaw.

"I don't know any girl," he cries out.

"Then why were you at the restaurant, watching him?" I nod my head toward Andrei.

"I was told to follow the future Brigadier," he whimpers, looking at Andrei in admiration. It's kind of funny as it's the same look so many men give

Andrei, like girls with crushes. "I am just doing what I was asked to do," he wails.

"You weren't following his girlfriend a few nights ago?" I lean closer and notice small drips of sweat accumulating on his forehead. He's nervous.

"No. This was my first time following him." He cries out in pain.

"Why are you following him though?" I throw my hammer back in my bag as the kid doesn't seem to be much of a threat. He's probably just someone's errand boy or a fan of Andrei.

"My boss heard there's a Savin in town. He wants to do business with the Coalition," the excitement in his voice irritates me. Definitely a fan boy.

Picking up on my eye roll and irritation, Andrei steps in, asking, "Who's your boss?" He holds up his hand to the kid when his phone begins to ring, then quickly dismisses the call.

Andrei stands tall in front of the kid with his hands crossed. "The professor. He runs drugs in this area," he answers calmly. He's finally stopped crying.

"The Savins aren't in the drug business. I think you're looking for the cartel."

The Savins view the drug business as beneath them, considering it an insult if anyone thinks they're associated with the street thugs who peddle substances people sniff up their noses.

"That's why he wants to meet. He wants to pull out of the drug business and has a proposition for you, the future leader of the Coalition."

"We'll pass." I wave him off and begin to cut him loose. He's wasting our time.

"Wait. Why do you call him the professor?" Andrei offers a hand to help him up.

Why is Andrei giving this kid the time of day? He's a low-level scumbag.

"He has a Ph.D. My boss is one of those smart guys, knows a lot about natural resources like oil and timber. He's also a professor at one of the universities," the kid calls out to us, still hoping to get our attention.

When I turn to Andrei, he's staring at the kid, interested.

"Tell your boss I'll meet him to hear what he has to say. But, under one condition. There's a threat around. I want your boss to see if there are new players in town besides us."

The kid shakes his head in excitement and when I raise my eyebrows toward the exit, he quickly runs out of the warehouse, yelling, "I'll pass the message to him."

"Natural resources?" I ask Andrei, laughing. *Is he for real?*

"We need to diversify. Spread the money around more. Natural resources, technology, lands ... it's a wide-open market the underground world hasn't tapped into yet."

Andrei and his brother Dmitri are good businessmen. I have never second-guessed their abilities to make all of us money by finding opportunities most underground players haven't even thought of.

I throw the bag back in the trunk when a ding sounds from my phone. Cora has messaged me. Now, I've become a message boy.

"My sister said to thank you for her roses," I say, passing on the message. "You didn't pick up her call."

"I didn't send her roses either," Andrei responds with his brows furrowed, looking irritable.

"You didn't send her these?" I hold up my phone to him with a picture of a dozen white roses sitting on her desk.

"No. I'm going to send her some tomorrow. I didn't have time yet. I came straight here after I dropped her off." His voice drifts off as he runs to the passenger seat, panicking.

"Call Cora and tell her not to touch them," he orders me as the vehicle speeds out of the warehouse and heads toward campus.

If those weren't from Andrei, then who sent them? Those roses were sent as a threat. Someone is close by. Someone who knew we weren't with Cora. And whoever sent them knows about Andrei's tradition of sending her those flowers.

Chapter Sixteen

CORA

The cherry blossoms are long gone, and the recent snow has melted. From my room window, I watch students running from dorms to classrooms as a downpour floods the streets.

Andrei and Sasha have turned me into a prisoner. It has been two weeks since I received the white roses that my boyfriend didn't send. Their fear of me getting hurt has locked me in my room. Michael escorts me to all my classes, and then I must return to staring at these four walls.

Even my coffee and food have to be delivered to me.

Feeling lonely, I walk back to my desk and stare at my laptop in front of me. Since I met with my professor, I've been working diligently on my application and paper for the writing program in London. Thoughts of walking its streets and experiencing such a diverse and creative culture bring me some joy. However, I somehow doubt the likelihood of ever leaving this room.

Worse still, I have yet to tell the guys about possibly studying abroad this summer. I know they'll say no, but I'll cross that bridge when I get there. First, I need to get accepted. Typing my final words, 'The End,' I submit my application.

Knock, knock. "It's Michael," I hear through the door before opening it.

"Andrei wants you to visit him tonight," he tells me, not attempting to hide a slight smirk.

I smile in excitement. I long to see my Andrei. It's also been two weeks since I last shared a bed with him. He and Sasha have been working late, dealing with the threats, running a few businesses, and being college students.

"Can you give me twenty minutes to get ready?" I ask, patting my hand against my yoga pants.

He nods, leaning against the wall, waiting for me outside. "I'll be here."

I know you will, I think, vexed as ever.

I quickly jump in the shower, run a straightener through my long hair, and apply makeup.

I rummage through my closet, snatching the first dress I see. When I catch my reflection in the mirror, disappointment washes over me. I want to look nice, to feel... how can I put it? Edible. Tantalizing. Irresistible!

So, I throw the dress on my bed and rifle through my closet again in a frantic search for something sexier. I find a tight black dress I wore to a party last semester and throw it on, feeling a bad girl vibe in me tonight. I glance at my high heels, but it's wet outside, so I grab a pair of sexy-heeled black boots that match my dress perfectly.

Giving myself one last look in the mirror, I'm ready. It's a little different than what I usually wear, but I want Andrei badly. I've longed for him and want him to desire me when I see him next.

"Ready!" I call to Michael, opening the door. His eyes widen as they move up and down my body as if devouring me with his eyes. When I tilt my head, he murmurs an apology. The first rule of security is that you don't look at the boss's girl as though she's eye candy. However, I give him a polite smile, letting him know I won't tell. We head out together to see Andrei.

I enter the apartment to find Sasha gone and a busy Andrei typing away at his desk. He doesn't even look at me when I say hello.

"Hey, Kitten. Give me a few more minutes. I've got some work to get done first," his voice trailing off as he continues to work, more or less ignoring me.

After my excitement of anticipation, I feel let down and deflated. But I don't say a word of complaint.

After a few minutes, he finally turns and glances at me with widened eyes. "That's a nice dress," he says, his predatory but flattering eyes locked on me.

"I haven't seen you much these past few weeks." I step closer to him, my fingers fidgeting behind my back.

He pulls out his chair to face me. "Take off all your clothes," he orders me abruptly. *Well, what was the sense in dressing for him?*

But despite his demand, I feel happy, my heart jumping at the excitement of him wanting me this way. With a big grin, I comply. Bending to unzip my boots when his voice cuts in, "No. Keep those on."

Slowly, I unzip my dress, pulling it over my head. I watch him watching me. There's a feeling of excitement at being watched. I toss my dress, then remove my bra. My nipples harden, and a pain begins to ache between my thighs. I slide my panties to the ground, feeling my own wetness on the fabric.

"Come here, Kitten." He spreads his legs open, and I crawl between his knees.

"I've missed you." He leans in, pressing his lips against mine. "Did you miss me?" he asks.

Biting my lower lip, I nod. I've thought about him every night alone in my room, often running my fingers between my pussy lips until I am soaked with my own juices.

Standing, he pulls me up, and I gasp at his strong force of a hold. His aggressiveness doesn't scare me. He only excites me more. With one hand, he pushes his laptop to the ground. He lifts my hips, placing my bare ass on his desk. With his hands around my ankles, he spreads my legs over his shoulders. My back arches backward as I try to hold myself up on my elbows. I pant in anticipation, our eyes locked on each other while he pulls his sweatpants down.

I grab his shirt and pull it over his head to showcase his lean, muscular body. Running my hand down his ripped abs, the ache between my legs becomes all of a sudden unbearable. My hot and needy pussy wants him so badly. Excited, I look into his eyes and moan his name, "Andrei."

He fists his cock with a few jerks before inserting his tip into me gently and perfectly. It seems so long ago that I was worrying whether he would even fit inside me. Now, we are like a jigsaw, a perfect fit, and he slides in far more easily than ever I would have believed, even though I am tight around his cock. Perfectly tight.

Maybe the ease is because my lips are already dripping for him, wanting, and craving his length. I slip my middle finger between my lips, then begin to rotate the tip of my finger around my clit.

His eyes move to me playing with myself. When he lets out a low growl, I tilt my head back and moan. His cock glides in me further as I inch my hips closer to him.

He grabs my waist and picks me up before falling into his office chair. I'm seated in his lap with his cock deep in me. Using my knees, I lift myself up and back down on his cock again, continuing to pound up and down as I ride every inch of him. His lips are fastened on my nipples, his muscled arms gripping me tight, making each thrust harder than before.

"Andrei! I'm about to come!" I scream as my breathing hardens.

"Hold it. Let's come together," Andrei moans breathlessly.

I squeeze my thighs to help ease my sensation. He's making it hard when he starts moving his waist into mine.

"Fuck!" Andrei screams out.

Those words escaping from Andrei's lips make my insides explode. Gripping my fingers around his neck, I scream my moans while he lets out a soft cry of pain at my nails puncturing his skin.

My middle takes in the warmth of his ceaseless spill into me. We sit there, soaked in each other, as we gently kiss, waiting for our pulses to come down from our orgasms.

His hands gently wipe my hair from my face, and I rest my head on his chest, my arms wrapped around his neck.

"Be ready to leave after your last class this week," he says.

"Where are we going?" I ask as he kisses my neck.

"Home." He kisses my cheeks before sucking my lips into his.

I'm completely caught off guard. "I wasn't planning on returning to New York for spring break."

"That's our home, Cora," he reminds me, but I'm fully aware of what New York is and the reason for not wanting to return there. I can't go back to my father after Andrei held a gun to his head on my behalf. My father will punish me for it when I'm alone with him.

"I can't see my father. I won't go home," I argue, attempting to pull away from him,

He grasps me gently but firmly on my upper arms, steadying me, reassuring me. "Hey ... hey ..." he says. "You surely do not think I would send you back there."

"Thank you," I whisper, overcome with fear, emotion, and gratitude to him.

"You're not going there, not ever. You're going home with me." He still grips me in his arms, holding me into him.

"Your parents are okay with me staying with you?" I've been to the Savins' home too often to count, but this time, it's different. This time, I'm no longer Sasha's twin sister. I'll be Andrei's girlfriend.

"Of course. My mom is excited to see you," he bites out as his lips nibble my chin.

I'm relieved. Andrei made a promise to protect me, and I knew when he did, he would stand by that promise.

He adds, "Plus, it's my father's birthday. We'll all be there for his dinner."

He lifts me to carry me to his room.

"Maybe I can try seeing my mom while we're home," I say. My talks with my mom have been strained since my dad's visit. I hope seeing her will relieve some of the tension between us.

"I'm sure Sasha can arrange for you to see her."

Laying me on his bed, he hovers over me. "Can we stop talking about our families so I can fuck you again and make you scream my name?"

Lifting my arms, I grab his headboard. Spreading my legs, I giggle. "Fuck me, Andrei."

Chapter Seventeen

ANDREI

"That's it?" my father yawns out. Leaning back in his chair, looking unimpressed.

"Brigadier, this has big potential," I state loudly as I flick off the presentation. I just introduced a plan that could potentially profit fifty million dollars in the next year as a trial run. If we find this new source of income lucrative, with more investment, we could make close to a billion dollars in ten years.

"You want us to invest in natural resources?" he asks.

Some of the Bratva's most influential and wealthiest men are sitting around the boardroom. So, I feel defeated when they start to laugh, especially when my father joins them.

Today isn't the first time I've presented a new money stream to them, but this is the first time I've asked them to invest in something they aren't familiar with.

Upset, Dmitri stands in front of the room full of Coalition bosses. We partnered on this project, and he owns it just as much as I do. "This, here, is exactly why we should invest," he says, gritting his teeth and pointing at all the men laughing at me.

Puffing a cloud of smoke across the table, my father asks with a challenge, "Okay, Dmitri. Tell us all about making money."

Dmitri might only be seventeen, but he's smart with business and numbers. Most people underestimate him because he has a killer instinct, like our brother Nikolai.

Dmitri ignores the snide remark, appearing as mature as the other men. He continues, "Men in the underground world have made loads of money through various means, as you know—drugs, weapons, women, government contracts, and other illegal activities. Because you've made so much money, you're content and happy with your current investments. But that doesn't mean that we can't do better. We should not be complacent."

I watch the men smirk. The men in this room are all billionaires, mostly obtained through illegal activities and funneled through the various legitimate businesses they own.

Dmitri continues, "For one thing, there are too many players in the same market. Bratva, Irish, Italians, and now the cartel is trying to take New York. What is the one thing you all have in common?"

"We're all bad men," one of the men shouts across the room and the room cheers.

"You are old bad men, too set in your ways. The world is changing." Dmitri seems to be getting their attention. They lean in closer, listening, waiting.

"Natural resources such as oil, timber, and land are an untapped market for the underground world. The Mafia is not investing in it. There's no dirty money being washed in that industry. So, guess what? The feds aren't watching." Dmitri steps aside, giving me the floor.

"Imagine if the Coalition, the Bratva, and our families were to get into the market now. We buy, invest, and make money before other underground players can think about it. We'll already have made billions of dollars by the time they invest. We'll be the pioneers into the industry for the Mafia." My lips move slowly, each word gaining more interest. However, my heart is pounding fast and loudly.

"And what do we know about natural resources?" My godfather, Brigadier Valentin, cuts in.

"Nothing. We've met someone in Seattle. He has a doctorate in this field. We'll be partnering up with him as our expert. Dmitri and I will be his liaisons." The words spill out of me faster than before, hoping I've still got their attention.

I watch my father and Valentin whisper to each other. The others patiently await their decision.

After what seems like forever, my father looks at me with no emotion. I just pray that he doesn't ridicule me in front of everyone.

"You'll be the future Brigadier one day. If you think this is smart, we'll make a small investment for now." He ends the discussion by smashing the lit side of his cigar into the ashtray.

I don't respond, still trying to hide my excitement.

After he adjourns the meeting, I watch my father shake the men's hands as they exit. My dad always stands out as the most dominant in a room full of powerful men.

Dmitri and I stand overlooking the city from the skyscraper. "It feels good to be home," I tell him. The busy streets and buildings are the view I want to wake up to every morning. I hate being in Seattle. It's still too green and wholesome for me there. I don't care about nature at all. But I'm not there for the outdoor adventures it offers. I'm there for her.

"It's nice to have you back," says Dmitri, his eyes moving across the skyline. He loves the city as much as I do. This is *our* home, and we plan to rule it together one day.

"That was a good speech, but did you really have to call them old?" I ask him.

We laugh silently so the men don't hear us.

A big grin crosses my brother's face. He knows he did good today. "It worked, didn't it?"

Seeing my father approach us, Dmitri begins to walk away, leaving me to have what I consider a winning moment with my dad.

At my young age, I consider myself a man. I run a billion-dollar business, work for the Bratva, and have killed. But standing next to my father, the man in me reverts to a little boy again. I see my father as a great dad, friend, protector, advisor, and inspiration. His most significant strength is his confidence.

"Natural resources, huh?" He joins me, his eyes piercing the city.

"Thanks for giving us a chance," I say, trying not to sound too eager. All I've ever wanted while growing up is to be like him.

"One day, all this will be yours," he says, dangling the city before me. I've heard this speech before.

"I know. I'm ready for it," I reply, trying to sound confident. I've been preparing to take my seat in the Coalition all my life, but can I ever measure up to him?

"Well, you say that, but as Vice-President, I need you at home here, in New York."

I knew he would bring this up. "I'm getting the job done in Seattle without any issues," I remind him. We have this same conversation every week since landing in Seattle.

My dad doesn't grasp technology and struggles to understand how I can run things online. We don't always have to meet in person, the old-school way of the Bratva.

"Son, I want you home here," he grumbles, but I'm not budging.

"Dad, you promised me one semester. Remember?" We argued when I told him I was leaving for Seattle. Reluctantly, he agreed to let me move.

"I figured now that you and Cora are together, you could move home now."

"That's not what Cora wants, though," I say, trying to sound like a man but feeling like a little kid asking my father to extend my curfew. "Anyway, we will move home together when our studies are done."

"You're a future Brigadier. She's in your possession now, so tell her what she wants." My dad doesn't understand her. If I push Cora too much, she'll run again.

"We aren't you and Mom. Our relationship is complicated." My dad didn't ask my mom to marry him. He told her she would be his wife, and that was a done deal. That's not the way I want to start my life with Cora.

"The men will see her as a weakness and use it against you," he insists, his harsh words hitting me. And he is correct; she is my weakness, but Sasha and I will always protect her.

"Then, they'll get dealt with by the Savin boys." My brothers promised me since we were little that they would protect her as though she was their own sister. In a way, she's the only girl we've ever had around, so it's an easy promise for them.

"Andrei, I want you home after the semester. No more messing around with the girl. You make her yours or leave her alone and let her live her life in Seattle. Do you understand me?" My father's stern voice makes it perfectly clear there's no room for argument.

"Yes, Dad." In that case, I'll need to return to New York this summer. I have a few months to convince Cora to come with me.

I'm excited to have Cora attend family dinner with me and wonder what she's been up to while I was in the city today.

"Now, let's head home before our guests arrive." He places his hand on my shoulder and I follow him out.

Did my father just say we have guests coming over? "What guests?" I ask him.

Chapter Eighteen

CORA

While the men are away at a business meeting, I settle in Andrei's room. When we were kids, I sometimes came in here to find Sasha. Running my hand across the sheets, I pause. *Things have changed a lot.* If you had asked me a few months ago if I would be sharing a bed with Andrei in the Savin home, I would have laughed while secretly wishing it were true.

I make my way down the bifurcated stairs into a spacious and impressive entry way. The Savin home is massive, its architecture exuding a sense of grandeur with its many lavish amenities. The estate has beautiful landscapes viewable from every window.

Of course, that same luscious view is obstructed by the many Savin soldiers guarding the property's perimeter. Sitting in between two other large estates owned by the Pakhan and Brigadier Valentin Volkov, this home has to be one of the safest places in New York. The guys left me here because it's the most secure place I can be.

With a book in my hand, I find the family room empty and sit in a chair overlooking Mrs. Savin's flower garden.

I used to sit here as a little girl, reading my books while Mom visited. Sasha and the Savin brothers would be outside this window playing football and running around the yard. Sometimes, I would just watch them, pretending to read my book. When they'd looked my way, I would quickly glance down at the pages, pretending not to notice them.

"You always loved reading in that window." A soft voice comes from behind me, making me jump.

"Hi! I love the view." I begin to stand, but Mrs. Savin waves her hands to gesture for me to sit.

Then she stands next to me, looking out the window, and after a long pause, she says, "It doesn't seem long ago that the boys played outside while you watched."

I'm so embarrassed she noticed!

She giggles and reflects, "Times have changed. You are all growing up way too fast."

Gently placing her hands on my shoulders, she leans down and kisses me on the top of my head. "Nice to have you home, Cora."

"I love this house. It's so beautiful here."

"One day, all this will be yours," she adds, catching me by surprise.

I know Andrei will inherit all his father's businesses and wealth when he becomes Brigadier. Still, I've truthfully never thought past my feeling of wanting Andrei. Does Mrs. Savin think her son and I have a future that might include marriage?

Since we were young, many of the daughters of Coalition men have been flirting and seeking out a relationship with Andrei. Being a future Brigadier and a Savin makes you royalty in our world. Andrei could snap his finger, and any of them would come crawling to him on their knees, hoping to become the Brigadier's wife.

I never thought about him that way. The plain fact was that little Andrei stole my heart the first time we met in this very room at the age of five. I've never seen Andrei for any of the material things he can offer his wife, only for the boy I've been longing for since we were kids.

I can't imagine owning all this. Before Andrei came to Seattle to be with me, I imagined staying there after college and doing my own thing. I just want a tiny home and to be able to write my stories. Now, I'm not sure what my future holds.

One of the housekeepers walks in, bringing Mrs. Savin and me something to drink. "I remember how much you loved your coffee, Miss Cora." She places the coffee beside me before walking away. *When did I become 'Miss Cora' instead of Cora?*

Something feels different about this visit. I have been coming here with my mother since I was five. Still, this time, housekeeping and security have been particularly attentive to me since I arrived, showing me the same respect they show the Savin family. I'm the first girl Andrei's brought home as a girlfriend; maybe they're just getting used to it as well.

"You should get ready for dinner. The men are almost home from the city," Mrs. Savin says as she hurries out of the room giving the housekeeper further instructions in Russian.

You don't take a car from the city to upstate New York when you're a Savin; you fly there in your helicopter. I wonder how their meeting went today, wishing I could ask. Andrei and Sasha do not share their business affairs with me, but I agree. The only thing I want from this life is for them both to make it home safely to me at the end of the day.

An hour later I receive a text from Andrei. He's home!

I glance at myself one last time before meeting him. Tonight is his father's birthday dinner, so I'm wearing a lovely black dress that ends halfway down my thighs. It's tight but not too revealing to have dinner with my boyfriend's parents.

The real surprise is what's underneath it. I ordered a see-through black bra and sheer underwear for when Andrei takes my dress off later tonight. *I can't wait!*

Running down the stairs to meet him and Sasha, familiar voices sound at the entrance. I come to a complete halt when I reach the bottom to see my parents talking to Mr. and Mrs. Savin. Both of them—Mom and Dad.

"You look absolutely beautiful." My mom walks over to me, embracing me in a hug.

"She always does," Mrs. Savin replies, admiring my dress.

Mr. Savin joins us, reaching out his hand. "It's good to have you home with us, Cora." He's always so polite for a man we all know is a ruthless killer.

Standing next to him is that cruel man who beat me and called me a slut the last time I saw him. "Dad." I don't run to him, don't embrace him. His glance back at me is as cold as if he doesn't know me from a lowly stranger in the street, as if I am someone he abhors.

"Cora," he says, uttering my name with such cruelty in his bite that it runs chills down my spine.

Scared, I retreat until I feel a body flush against me, instantly relaxing when his hands grab mine, interlocking our fingers. He whispers, "Sorry, I didn't have time to warn you."

Standing there, Andrei and my father glare at each other, neither of them bothered by the fact that everyone in the room is watching them.

"Let's head into the dining room and have some wine," Mrs. Savin cuts in. She and my mother begin their gossip session about the other ladies as they leave the room.

My father follows, eyes narrowing on me, ignoring Andrei and Sasha standing behind me.

"Did something happen that I need to know about?" Mr. Savin quietly asks Andrei, his eyes glancing at me.

"No," Andrei replies. I'm sure my pale face is telling him quite a different story.

I hadn't realized before that I had been holding my breath the entire time I was in the same room as my father. I'm drawn back to Andrei when I hear him click the safety button on his gun. A sigh of relief escapes me, comforted by the knowledge that Andrei intends to keep his promise to never let my father hurt me again.

Chapter Nineteen

CORA

"The best birthday present I received this year is having you kids home," Mr. Savin toasts to Andrei and Sasha. Mr. Savin's love for Sasha is genuine. I've watched over the years how he's considered him one of his boys, taking him on family vacations and including him in their many celebrations. Looking at my brother, he's also happier here with the Savins than he is at home with our parents.

I look at my father, but he's too busy watching Sasha.

"What are the plans for summer?" Mrs. Savin asks us.

"We'll come back here to New York. I've got business to deal with in the city. Sasha and Cora will join me," Andrei replies.

My father's eyes burn into me with a fierce glare. I have no desire to return and be near him. The way he's looking at me right now makes me uncomfortable and urges me to flee.

"Actually, I'll be spending the summer in London," I say, speaking up for myself.

"What?" Andrei questions me.

"I got accepted to a writing program in London this summer."

I avoid eye contact with Andrei and Sasha, already feeling their gazes piercing through me. My acceptance letter arrived only this morning. I didn't want to reveal it here, but Andrei has no right to make summer plans for me.

I'm not going to just follow him wherever he leads. I have things to do on my own.

"I won't allow it!" Andrei slams his fist against the table, catching me by surprise.

I gasp, "Excuse me? You don't get to tell me what to do."

"We're trying to protect you, and you think we'll allow you to travel around the world to attend a few classes?"

I looked to Sasha for backup but didn't get it. He's in agreement with Andrei.

"I don't have to ask you for permission to live my life how I want to, Andrei," I insist, raising my voice. I'm embarrassed we are having this conversation in front of our parents, but he can't be allowed to think he can control me and meet with no resistance.

My dad cuts in. "Actually, you do need his permission to go."

"What?"

He doesn't respond but sits there enjoying our little show with a grin from ear to ear. *Asshole!*

"What is he talking about?" I ask around the room. No one is looking directly at me. It's as if there's some inside joke, but I am the only one not included in it.

Again, my dad laughs. "Now that you two are together, I thought Andrei would have told you."

"Keep your mouth shut," Andrei snaps, scowling at him.

My father raises his voice. "Now, is that how you want to start your relationship? With a big secret?"

Standing up, I yell across the table, "What secret?"

Mr. Savin raises his hands and asks me nicely, "Cora, sit." Even in my state of anger, I know better than to disobey his orders. The rest of the room falls silent. "Cora, you and Andrei will marry when you turn twenty-one."

"What do you mean?" I ask him but already know the answer.

"It was decided for you when you were young." He's calm and collected.

"Why?" I turn to face my parents, both silent. The only difference is that my mother can't look me in the eye. She stares away as if there is something fascinating through the window.

"Your dad and I had a business arrangement. You are payment for that deal," Mr. Savin finishes.

Of course, I know all about arranged marriages in the underground world and should have realized it far sooner. Fathers trade their daughters to forge alliances with other families. My mother and Mrs. Savin were both married through arrangements.

But times have changed. Society today has given women so much independence that the underground world needs to accept it and no longer treat us like commodities. We are people, people with feelings.

"You knew about this as well?" I ask Sasha.

"No. But, I've been suspecting it for a long time," he answers.

I let out a soft cry, placing my hand over my mouth. This explains so much. In high school, when boys talked to me, they were immediately threatened by the Savin brothers and Sasha because Andrei didn't allow it. Now, it is clear that they weren't protecting me. They were saving me for Andrei. I was owned from the beginning and never did have a choice.

I turn to Andrei, "But you knew about the arrangement."

"Cora ..." Andrei places his hand over mine, and I quickly pull away.

"Don't touch me!" I cry out. I don't want to cry in front of everyone, but I can't stop the water from leaving my eyes.

When Andrei came to Seattle, I thought it was because he liked me and wanted to be with me. His betrayal hurts deeply, destroying my trust. *I've been such a fool!*

I now understand why my father hates me, why he hits me and calls me insults. Because to him, I am just a commodity to trade. I look at my father with disgust. The sad part is that the look he gives me back is one of a father who couldn't care less that he's caused me this pain.

Feeling exposed, vulnerable, and insecure, no longer able to trust any of these people, I run from the table as fast as my feet will move.

Taking two steps at a time, I run straight for Andrei's room, not because I feel safe there but because I don't know where else to go. Inside, I slam the door, letting out the loudest screams of frustration, not caring who hears me.

Today is the day I found out I'm owned.

Chapter Twenty

CORA

I don't' know how long I've sat here, my head down on Andrei's desk as tears and snot run down my face. I lift my head to blow my nose. That's when I find a picture on Andrei's desk. A picture I hadn't noticed until now, that of my sixteen-birthday party. We were so young in the photo. That night meant everything to me.

***

Mr. Savins' office was off limits to the party, so there was some intimacy in there without the hundred high school students just outside the door.

I sat there on his father's desk with my legs spread apart as Andrei inched closer to me. With his finger, he moved my hair from my eyes and tucked it neatly behind my ear. "Cora," he said, his mouth a few centimeters from mine.

My heart sped up. I'd been imagining this for years. I had watched, waited for, and wanted Andrei. And now, at this moment, I had him.

Closing my eyes, I opened my mouth to feel everything he was willing to give me. Our two hearts beat fast, and the moment we'd both wanted had come. It was so close it made me feel like it had already happened.

Just when he went to press his lips against mine, a loud voice cut in. "There you two are. I've been looking for you both. Let's take a selfie. I want to remember this night."

My drunken twin brother had stumbled into the room. Andrei quickly pulled away from me as he embraced Sasha in a hug.

"Dude, you are so wasted," Andrei said, wrapping his arms around Sasha's neck.

"Who isn't? This is the best birthday party. My brother, thank you." Sasha kissed Andrei on the forehead.

"Picture?" Andrei grabbed the phone. Both boys wrapped their arms around me as Andrei held the phone up in the air and snapped the image they wanted.

Andrei glanced at me, smirking, making me laugh in response. Sasha was so drunk that we both hoped he wouldn't notice the two of us had been about to kiss when he walked in.

"Shots! We need shots!" Sasha enthused, grabbed Andrei and pulled him away from me and back into the party, leaving me alone for the rest of the night.

***

Now, everything I see shines back through a different set of eyes, a new worldview on everything I believed I understood.

"That was such a great party," Sasha sneaks up behind me, killing my memory, just like he killed my chance of getting a kiss that night.

"For you, it was," I mumble, annoyed, then I put the picture of the three of us back where I found it.

"I can't believe he still has that picture." Sasha places his two big arms around me, squeezing me into a tight hug. I'm mad at him right now but also longing for someone's support, and he is the only one who has come to placate me.

"He has a lot of pictures of the two of you around here."

"He didn't keep that picture because I'm in it."

Sasha leans down, kissing the top of my head in an attempt to comfort me, but the person I truly need right now is the one I just discovered has betrayed me.

"I hate that night." I try to push the memory away and walk over to the bed.

"Yes, I remember. The night you desperately wanted Andrei to kiss you," he teases me.

"What?" He was too drunk to notice, wasn't he? Did Andrei say something to him?

He chuckles, adding, "Sis, I was drunk, not blind."

"So, you know he didn't kiss me then." I had dreamed about that moment for months, replaying it in my head, imagining what his kiss would have felt if it had come to fruition.

"Good memories. You know he threw that party just for you."

"Don't be silly. It was for you. I'm just the twin sister who tagged along." I wish my brother would stop the fakeness. I now know Andrei is only with me because of an obligation.

"Are you kidding me? We had my party the night before at the Gentleman's Club. Brigadier Valentin bought me my first private show," he says, sounding too excited. I don't want to imagine what the guys did at that club that night.

"It was all because of Andrei. He wanted you to have a sweet sixteen, like all of the other Coalition girls. Father wouldn't let Mom throw one, so Andrei did."

I think back to how surprised I was. That party was the best I've ever had. And there must have been about a thousand white roses around the house.

Sasha stands there as though not knowing what words to say next but finally lets out a sigh. "Cora, the Savins have considered you family for a long time. They've been taking care of you since you were little."

I think back to when we were small, back to how Mrs. Savin always showed me kindness above the other little girls. Mr. Savin always went out of his way to say hello to me when he wouldn't address any other kids around the room. Then, it falls in place ... The clues were always there, even the brothers, who were always watching and protecting me.

He continues, "Your security guards, private schools, college tuition, everything you've ever wanted, they are the ones who paid for it."

I never asked for any of those things, only believing my parents were providing for me, but nothing was what it seemed.

Since I was a little girl, I've been in love with Andrei. I'm still in love with Andrei. My feelings haven't changed, although I have always wanted him to love me back. For a time, it almost seemed that he did. The difference now is that I'm not confident Andrei likes me because of who I am rather than because he's been told to.

And that feeling is the hurt that hits you in the gut and rips your heart out. Now, I am beginning to wish I had never let myself fall so hard for him. It feels as if I have made a fool of myself.

"Hey." My brother's warm hand rests on mine for a second, his voice breaking into my reverie. "Talk to Andrei." His words trail off as he leaves me alone to cry again.

Chapter Twenty-One

ANDREI

I saw the look on Mr. Belov's face when Cora got upset. He clearly orchestrated this mess, which I can only assume was payback for holding a gun to his head. He wants Cora to hate me. He got his wish.

My only apprehension in telling her about our prospective marriage was to protect her. I wanted to win her heart before she knew she belonged to me anyway.

Just as Cora has now been told, she was promised to me when we were children as payment from her father to mine. Her arrogant father had almost bankrupted the family when he'd tried to diversify the family's business portfolios, even when his advisors had cautioned him against being so aggressive. But, eager to make money, her father had invested in businesses and stocks that became worthless, just the way he'd been warned.

Embarrassed and ashamed, her father secretly met with mine. My dad agreed to lend him money at a cost. There would be a price, and Cora was it.

Our mothers grew up together and were always friends. My mother said she had seen something in Cora early on and thought she would be a good pick for a future Savin wife. So, when Cora's father needed help, my father agreed on one condition, that Cora be promised to me, his eldest son and future Brigadier.

On the day Cora and I are to wed, her stakes in her family's businesses and fortune will finally be transferred to the Savin family, the day when it all is made good again, a debt repaid—with interest. But of course, it hasn't all been smooth sailing because her greedy and manipulative father has always accused my father of being unfair.

Her mom though, she loves the idea, excited by the thought of her daughter becoming a Brigadier's wife. It's only because of this that her father agreed to go through with it. He was desperate, and desperate men do desperate things.

Our parents had an agreement. On our thirteenth birthdays, we would learn all about our arranged marriage. Since my birthday fell a few months before Cora's, I was the first to know about the arrangement.

But I knew Cora would not feel the same way about being a debt payment. She wouldn't like it.

She was shy and delicate, and I didn't want to lose her before we even had a chance to be together, so I asked them to keep our marriage arrangement a secret until she got older.

The two of us were just kids, and adulthood seemed like a lifetime away. Besides, I was a teenage boy and not yet ready to love Cora. So, I left her on the sideline to watch while I indulged in my bad boy ways in high school, including enjoying other girls.

I'm a selfish bastard, always have been, and didn't allow Cora the same freedom or enjoyment. High school boyfriends—she had none.

Cora had also wanted out. She wanted to be away from New York City and our life. So, when her father asked me permission to allow Cora to attend college in Seattle, I agreed out of guilt.

But I missed her, of course, and should have seen it coming.

When I saw her that night, a surge of emotions overwhelmed me, and I couldn't bear to stay away. It was time to put my mark on her and make her truly mine. That night in her bedroom changed everything. I had tasted her, setting a dangerous precedent, especially if she would no longer be around New York City.

I wanted more of it, needed it, craved it. There was no way to be in New York and not around her, so what followed was inevitable.

I followed her to Seattle, knowing it was time I grew up and did the right thing. It was time to claim the girl who stole my heart when we were kids.

***

I entered the room to find a little girl my age sitting there holding a book. "Who are you?" I'd never seen her before today. I would remember if I had.

Her beautiful eyes gazed into mine. "Cora Belov," she replied shyly.

Cora. What a beautiful name for a gorgeous girl. She must have been my new friend Sasha's twin sister. He'd told me about her.

"I'm Andrei Savin," I said in a way I hoped was impressing her. Why was I nervous?

"This is where you live?" she asked.

"Yes. This is where we come when we're not in the city." I tried not to sound arrogant, even if it was the truth.

She didn't respond, her hands gripping her book as if she were afraid of me. Oh, no! That wasn't the first impression I wanted to make.

"What are you reading?" I asked in hopes of making her feel comfortable.

"It's a book about kittens," she said and smiled, and her shoulders dropped.

"Why kittens?" I didn't read unless required at school, so I couldn't understand why she would read a book for fun.

"Because they're adorable, soft, and warm. I always wanted one, but my dad's allergic." Soft and warm like the girl who sat in front of me.

My friend Sasha burst into the room, "Andrei, come outside. We're about to play football."

"I'm coming," I told him. Before I left the room, I looked back at the little girl staring at me and knew she was special.

***

"Andrei," a soft voice catches my attention.

"Kitten." I jump up from my chair excitedly. I wanted to run after her earlier, but my father told me to give her space.

"I'm not sure how I feel right now."

She doesn't come to me. She's distant. I can't blame her. "Take the time you need," I say.

I've only felt fear a few times in my life, and right now is one of those moments. I'm the future Brigadier, raised to be a ruthless, tenacious, and confident leader. But not knowing if Cora plans to leave me makes me feel like a desperate boy.

"Come." I stand from the chair, waiting for her. I need her near me.

As she walks over, she reminds me of the shy little girl I once knew. Tonight, we've taken from her the self-confident woman she had grown into.

Gripping her face in my hands, I hold her tight. "Cora, you mean everything to me. Please don't leave me."

"Do you understand how I feel?" She attempts to pull away from me, but I grip her harder, unable to let her go.

I can't imagine how she feels right now. Arranged marriages are part of the underground world. I don't care for it, but it's a tradition our parents believe in and live themselves. Even though the marriage was thrust upon us, Cora was given to me as payment. In this life, it's the women who are the true victims.

"Dmitri and I closed a big deal today," I tell her, confiding in her. We aren't supposed to talk about work with our women.

"You want to change the subject to work?" So, I've upset her more, but that wasn't my intention.

"Listen," I whisper, trying to get her to calm down and hear me out. "We closed a deal to invest in natural resources in Seattle. We are trying to change the Coalition and show there's money in other commodities besides women. We are creating a more diverse Bratva than the men currently running it."

"That's a big step, Andrei." Her voice is still subdued, but at least she's speaking to me. Cora understands the Bratva. She knows we're evil men who do bad things.

"Lead by my side," I tell her. "I want to be the change in the Bratva. Help me do that."

"How?" she asks me, tilting her head quizzically.

"We can start by not trading daughters as payment for business deals. When we have our daughter, yours and mine, we'll let her choose who she loves." Her eyes beam. I'm unsure if it's because I asked her to help me or the mention of us having kids together.

"I can support that." She continues, "I don't want you to marry me because you were told you must, though. I want a husband who wants to love me till our dying days."

People say we don't know what love is when we're kids. But I knew the first moment I saw her, *my kitten*. "You belong to me. You always have. You always will."

"I love you, Andrei," she whispers.

I know she does. She always has. But, for some reason, I can't say those words back to her. Grabbing her face between my palms again, I assure her,

"I don't know if a man like me, who was raised to be a killer, can give you the kind of love you deserve. But I'm going to work hard trying."

She musters a faint smile.

"Now, take off that dress, and let me see what you're wearing under it." My cock has been hard since I saw her come down the stairs in her pretty dress.

"Andrei, we're in your parents' living room," she glances around.

"You mean our living room. This is our future home, and I can't wait to come home to you every night." I kiss her, taking the last of her air.

Chapter Twenty-Two

CORA

It's only been a month since I returned from New York. While Andrei and Sasha are busy working, I've continued to be a locked bird in a cage, and the quietness and boredom give me too much time to think.

I replay Mr. Savin's dinner repeatedly in my head, thinking of my father's smirk when I found out I had been promised as payment. There was no comfort, no sorry, no remorse. The worst part was my mother sitting there silently. *Is this what the Bratva does to you?* It takes away any compassion for life in exchange for power and money.

"Come on! It will be fun," Nicole begs me, twirling around the room in one of my borrowed dresses. I don't remember her asking, but I haven't said anything all year on any occasions I've seen her wearing something out of my closet. Honestly, I'm not sure if she's returning them after each 'borrow,' but I can buy new ones. She's been trying to get me to attend a frat party with her tonight.

Moving away from the window, I pick up my book and settle into bed. "You know I can't," I respond.

She doesn't know about Andrei's life but has noticed that I've been staying in since he's been my boyfriend.

"Don't let some asshole control you." Walking over to my closet, she ruffles through my wardrobe until she picks out a black dress.

"Changing?" I ask her.

"Nope. This is what you are wearing tonight." Throwing a dress I had recently bought for a private dinner with Andrei down on the bed next to me. It was a little too revealing for my taste with holes around my hips and shoulders, but it drove Andrei crazy.

The last time I wore something of value was in New York. I pinch my sweatshirt and bring it up to my nose. *Jeez! Maybe she's right!*

I'm only allowed to go to class, the coffee shop, and back to my dorm. 'Allowed.' Most women would take offense to that word, and I do too, but in our world, it's customary.

Now that I know I've been promised to Andrei and that one day I will be a Brigadier's wife, things are different. My perspective on my situation is beginning to shift. Every day, there will be a threat to my life because of who I'll be marrying, rendering me a pawn in a game in the underground world, the prize being Andrei Savin's death.

But we're young, still just teenagers. For now, Mr. Savin is still their family's leader, and I came to Seattle merely to be a college student, not a Coalition wife.

What's the harm in a bit of college fun, right?

I fold down the corner of the page to mark my spot, then throw the book down. "So, where is this party?" I ask Nicole.

"At Adam's frat," she responds, blending in the pink blush on her pale cheeks.

I went to Adam's fraternity house many times last semester when I was his girlfriend. I feel safe there, and Adam and I have remained friends, so attending a party is appealing. Grabbing the black dress, I begin to get ready. "Okay, but just for a little while."

She beams and claps. "We're going to have so much fun!"

Across campus, Nicole and I enter the frat house and are met with a whistle from Adam. "I didn't think I would see you at another frat party," he says with his frat boy charm.

After scanning the room, he asks me, "No brother or boyfriend tonight?"

"I am a grown woman who can come to a party when I feel like it," I retort with a furrowed eyebrow, even though I know my statement is a lie.

"In that case, let's have some fun tonight. Like old times." Adam grabs Nicole and me a cup of jungle juice, and we begin to sip and talk.

It feels nice to laugh and not have the stress of the Coalition or what my future holds. *I miss this!* I miss having the freedom to be a college student and have fun. I didn't get to do this much in high school either; college was supposed to be my do-over. And it was until Sasha and Andrei showed up.

A few jocks bump into me as they carry another keg into the kitchen. "Keg stand?" Adam asks.

I give him a surprising look, my finger pointed to my chest. "Me?"

"Yeah! You've never done one and always said you wanted to try it." The crowd cheers me on.

"You go first, then I'll do it," Nicole pushes me toward the keg.

"I don't know how to do this," I laugh.

"Hold on to this." Adam points to the keg handles. I grasp each one and bend at the waist as two guys fling me upside down into a handstand. Adam pours beer into my mouth. *It's fucking disgusting!*

The crowd yells, "Drink it! Drink it!" as the beer gushes down my throat.

I can see Nicole laughing and cheering me on. The beer gushes down my throat and I'm relieved with the frat boys turn me back over until my feet hit the floor. My head spins in agony, and I immediately know it was a mistake.

Nicole wraps her arms around me, and I whisper in her ear, "I'm drunk!"

"Have fun tonight. I'll take care of you." We both stand there hugging so she can hold my body up while watching a few more girls take their turn upside down.

Looking past Adam, I find a familiar face watching me. He's one of the frat boys. Then remember my brother talking to him last time I was here. *Crap!*

"I need to go to the bathroom," I yell at Nicole over the loud music and stumble down the hall. Two girls bump into me coming out of the bathroom, but I wave them off in a rush. I quickly attempt to shut the door, but a foot stops it from closing. I open it slightly and see the Russian guy standing there.

"You need to go home now."

"I don't take orders from you." I do the only thing I can, kick his foot and close the door. After using the toilet, I stare at myself for a few minutes, already seeing a few drops of sweat on my forehead as my body heats up from the large amount of liquor consumed. I need to find Nicole so I can go home before the guys show up and hurt Adam.

When I exit the bathroom, the same guy is waiting for me. "I said leave me alone," I tell him. But he doesn't listen; instead, he grabs my arm. Trying to shake him off is pointless because his grip is unyielding.

Nicole and Adam notice my struggle and rush over to help me. "Cora, is this guy bothering you?" Adam asks.

My brother's associate responds, "Back off. This isn't your business."

Adam pushes him, and he stumbles backward, tripping over a few students. By now, a crowd of partygoers is watching us.

"Let's get out of here." Nicole guides me out of the party with Adam to a car I don't recognize.

"Whose car is this?" I ask him because I know he doesn't own one.

"A friend. Let me get you girl's home." He sounds sincere, and I know my friends will keep me safe.

I pause to look at the guy running out of the house towards us wondering why he's so persistent in bothering me tonight.

"Get in the car." Adam grabs my arm, and my muscles immediately feel bruised. This no longer feels right.

"Let go of me." I attempt to pull away.

Adam begins pushing me into the backseat.

"Adam," I scream, trying to get him off me. The next thing I feel is my head hitting the car doorframe before my eyes slowly close.

I hear the engine and laughter in the air. My head hurts, and I'm confused and disoriented. The last thing I remember is Adam being aggressive with me. I must have passed out drunk and dreamt it. I know Adam, and he wouldn't do that to me. Plus, Nicole was there, and Nicole is my friend. I gradually come to, opening my eyes slowly.

I'm lying in the back of a car and can barely see Adam driving. I squint through the dark car toward the woman's voice, finding Nicole in the passenger seat. When she notices me looking at her, she tells him, "She's waking up."

I want to ask what's happening, but I can't speak. *What's going on?*

Adam looks back at me. "This will all be over soon, Cora," he says before kissing Nicole.

Chapter Twenty-Three

ANDREI

"It's been quiet, and that worries me," I grumble to Sasha. Since returning from New York, Cora hasn't received any threats. In our world, that usually means something bigger is coming.

"Are you sure there's a plane arriving?" Sasha asks.

There's been an unusual amount of noise from New York here in Seattle. Our new partnership with the professor has given us access to the underground world in the Pacific Northwest, access we didn't have before. One of his men informed us that a plane, not on the manifest, will land shortly. We could be chasing a dead-end lead, or the person getting off this plane could be the one who threatened Cora and is moving against my family. Either way, it has Sasha and me standing outside a private airport near Seattle, shivering in the cold darkness.

"I hate this fucking place," Sasha repeats. He likes to remind me of that fact as much as possible. He sticks his hands in his pockets, and his shoulders hunch over, shivering from the cold.

"Me too, my friend." Seattle is nowhere near any place we've dreamt of visiting. I'm sure Cora picked it because it was on the opposite end of the continent from New York. I hadn't realized how much I hurt her in high school until she decided on the farthest place to attend college.

A hum enters the air space, catching our attention as a private plane comes in for landing. We retreat further into the dark to hide.

Patiently, we wait. When the doors open, we immediately notice who it is.

When the last man appears at the door, I shoot a look at Sasha, and he looks like he's seen a ghost. "What the fuck is he doing here?" I ask him.

"I don't know," he replies, just as stunned as I am, pulling out his cell from his pocket and dialing a phone number he knows too well.

The man on the other end answers, "Hello, Sasha!"

"Hey, Dad. I called to check in on you after our night at the Savins' home," Sasha whispers, not to draw attention to us. I hold my ear close to the phone to hear his response.

"We are good, son." We watch his father smiling as he walks down the stairs toward the vehicle waiting for him. A few men are with him who don't usually belong to his security detail.

"When do you plan to visit Seattle again?" Sasha asks.

"Not anytime soon." *Fucking liar!*

"Have a good night, Dad." Sasha's eyes are saddened as he realizes his father has lied to him. What other secrets does Sasha not know about?

"Goodnight too, Son." Then, a click.

We both look at each other in disbelief. Sasha's father wouldn't be stupid enough to move against a Brigadier, would he? He grew up in the Coalition along with my father. Although he isn't as high-ranking as Dad, he is high-ranking enough to know that starting a war against the Savins is a death wish.

I watch my best friend. He's been crossed. I have never questioned Sasha's loyalty, but I now wonder if he would side with me against his father.

Sasha's phone keeps going off, and we can't afford any more surprises tonight. "Sasha, who keeps texting you? It's getting fucking annoying."

He takes his phone from his pocket and reads the messages. "We have an issue."

"It can wait. We have a bigger problem right now." I need to call my dad.

"It seems your future wife, my sister, decided to have fun at Adam's frat house tonight."

I know we've kept Cora locked up, but now that she knows the truth, that she is a future Brigadier's wife, she would understand and obey my orders. She always was a little defiant, though, not taking orders and constantly reminding us that this world is our life, not hers. "Send Michael to retrieve her," I order.

"There's a problem. Cora's roommate Nicole and Adam put her in a car an hour ago, and our friend lost contact with her." I'm hoping her friends are taking care of her, but something about this whole night has made me nervous. Call it gut instinct.

Fuck! "This isn't what I need right now." Of all the times, Cora chooses to enjoy a night of college life.

We follow Mr. Belov across the city, making sure to keep enough distance between the two vehicles to go unnoticed. When his vehicle enters a warehouse, we pull over at the end of the street hidden by a dark alley. There's already a car waiting, and I wonder who he's meeting.

A tall guy gets out with a baseball cap, and I can't believe it when he turns around. I know exactly who he's meeting with. *Adam!* Also, getting out of the vehicle is Cora's roommate, Nicole. Now, this is quite a surprise.

Adam leans into the back of the car and then stands with an unconscious woman in his arms. *Cora!*

"What the fuck?" I panic, grabbing the door handle to run to her. That fucker better not have hurt her. My heart skips, not knowing what they may have done to her. But she's alive. At least, I hope so.

Sasha grabs my arm, stopping me from exiting the car. "Call your dad. We'll need backup."

Sasha's right. I pull out my phone, snapping a picture of Adam standing beside Mr. Belov with Cora slung over his shoulders.

'Dad! Send help!' I text him and my brothers.

Our computer guys have a tracker on my phone, so my dad knows where all his sons are. If Cora has her phone on her, he'll be able to track her as well.

"Ready?" I ask Sasha.

I place a new clip into my gun, stepping into the dark night air, ready to run to her. But we haven't made it far when we're met by a flank of men behind us, guns in hand, pointed at us.

I hope my dad makes it on time!

Chapter Twenty-Four

CORA

The pounding in my head is unbearable. I can't entirely open my eyes. Raindrops can be heard hitting the metal roof and the sun begins to shine through the high windows. I lift my arm and rub the back of my head, which aches with pain. *Where am I?*

A man's voice is audible not too far away from me, a familiar voice in a language I know too well. *Russian!*

I lie still for a moment, believing I'm imagining someone or dreaming. Pulling myself upright, I finally have enough energy to sit up. My hand runs over my face, and I slowly open my eyes. "Dad?"

"Cora," he says. Why would my dad be here? The last thing I remember is Adam forcing me into the car and seeing him kiss Nicole. I got so drunk last night. I must be imagining this.

The image of a man walking toward me becomes clearer, and it is my dad; there is no mistaking him. Looking around, I find myself on a couch in the middle of a warehouse. "What's going on?"

Men who work for my dad fills the space, moving about, ignoring me. I find my dad talking to someone I've seen before, but I don't really know. With my arms crossed, I walk over to my father. "Dad, answer me!"

"Be quiet and stop acting like a child," he scolds me. His dark eyes narrow on me, reminding me I'm nothing to him.

"Dad, tell me what's going on now!" I scream at him. Suddenly, the back of his hand hits my cheek, sending my body flying backward.

I am not his rag doll any longer. He cannot continue to treat me like a child. I find the strength deep in me, and in a fit of rage, I attack him with my closed fist. When my knuckles are about an inch from his face, a hand grabs my wrists, pulling me back, flying me across the floor, and my ass hits the ground.

The man who grabbed me looks down at me like I'm a piece of garbage on the floor.

It takes me a minute to get back on my feet, my head still heavy from drinking. "Who are you?" I ask, rubbing my wrist to ease the pain and eyeing him with disdain.

He brings his face to mine and with a conspiratorial smirk he replies, "Your future husband."

I gasp. "You must be confused. I'm already engaged to someone else." Even if I hadn't been promised to Andrei, I would never consider marrying a man who does business with my father.

My father looks unbothered that this man just threw me to the ground.

"Change of plans, Cora," my father announces. "You will be marrying Boris, my new business partner."

"Dad, you know I'm promised to Andrei," I remind him as though he doesn't remember. When I last saw him, he made it a big deal, trying to cause me to hate Andrei.

"Yes, but your Andrei will be dead soon, and you will be available for another suitor."

Dead? He said 'dead soon' so Andrei's alive and if he's alive he's on his way to save me.

Then I remember my phone. I rub my hand on my dress still feeling my phone tucked into the open slit of my dress. I'm not stupid enough to think my phone doesn't have a tracker, but for the first time, I'm happy it does.

Disgusted by the two men in front of me, I turn to avoid them, only to run straight into my biggest enemies: Adam and Nicole. *Assholes! This must have been planned last night.* When I finally made friends, I should have known they were in it for the wrong reasons. This is why 'we' keep our circle close. I won't make this mistake again.

I'm very familiar with how the underground world works. In all my years sitting in the corner reading my books, I paid attention. No one does anything for free.

"So, what's in it for you two?" I ask Adam and Nicole, the words hissing between my teeth, sounding like the snakes they are.

With a smug smile, Adam replies, "Money, of course. Your father offered me a job."

"And what exactly was the job?" I ask him, but I already know the answer.

"To fuck you!" His words are just as disgusting as the little boy in front of me.

"Why?" I turn and ask my dad.

"I figured if you weren't a virgin, Andrei wouldn't want a slut for a wife. But I underestimated your love for the boy. I never saw it coming that you would save yourself for him. You're even more stupid than I thought. And when he and your brother came running to Seattle after you, I knew I'd need to kill him."

I hate him and loathe the sight of him.

"You promised me to Andrei. So, why are you doing this?" This makes no sense. My dad is the one who entered into an agreement with Mr. Savin about our arranged marriage.

"Cora. You don't understand our world. When you marry Andrei, half of my business and money will belong to the Savins. You think I would let those privileged fuckers own what I built?" A pain shoots through my heart. No one told me I came with a monetary bonus.

I look over to someone I opened up to, someone I trusted. "So, what's in it for you?" I ask Nicole, my eyes watering.

She smiles. "Cora, you don't understand what being poor is like. Your entire life, you were a princess. And like a princess, you've been promised to a future king. But I had to fend for myself and going to college meant massive loans. So, when your father asked me to spy on you in exchange for my college tuition, I agreed. Sleeping with Adam was a bonus."

She doesn't take her eyes off me when she leans in toward Adam, and he kisses her passionately in a way he never kissed me. *Bitch!*

"You're the threat to the Savins?" I ask my dad. This also means my father had someone follow me and scare me. *He's a sick bastard!*

"When Andrei and Sasha find out, you're all dead!" I scream out to the warehouse.

My father pulls out a cigar from his coat and lights it up. As he walks over to me, he stops just a few inches away and blows the smoke into my face. We stand there, neither of us showing any emotion toward the other. Then he gives me the biggest smirk I've ever seen when he holds his hand up in the air, waving to the soldiers.

The soldiers return to the room with two men I recognize, even with their hands tied and faces covered by plastic bags.

Boris finds pleasure in uncovering the guys' heads. I begin to cry. It is Andrei and Sasha, and my world has caved into this sudden realization. *No one is coming to save us!*

Chapter Twenty-Five

CORA

I scream and start running to Andrei, but an arm wraps around me, pulling me away from him. My eyes meet a boy I trusted not too long ago, but now I find his smile upsetting and aggravating. "Do not touch me again."

"Don't touch her," Andrei echoes behind me.

Adam is trying to act tough, but behind his smug smile, I can see that he's realized he's in over his head. Boys grow up thinking it's cool to be a bad guy, lured in by the allure of women, money, and power. But that's the superficial part of the underground world. In reality, you wake up every day not knowing if it will be your last. It's a life of violence, cruelty, and death. You can only trust those closest to you; even then, they can become your worst enemies. My eyes turn to my father.

"Dad, Sasha is your son!" I yell at him.

"He made his choice when he chose the Savin family over ours," he voices with disdain in his eyes when he glances over to my brother.

"He's a Belov. You can't kill him!" He surely wouldn't kill his own son, to whom he's been promising to leave his legacy.

"Let's see if he's still a Belov." My father walks over to Sasha and unties the rope around his wrists. He gestures for Boris' gun and places it between Sasha's hands, guiding his fingers around the trigger. Turning Sasha around, my father points the weapon at Andrei's head.

"If you are still my son, the future heir to the Belov fortune, pull the trigger. Get rid of this Savin asshole, and you can rule by my side, Son." The way he spits out 'son' is nothing but venomous, true hatred residing in his stare.

To further mock my brother, my father kisses Sasha on the forehead like any father would after giving his son advice and comfort.

Sasha doesn't pull the trigger. His hands shake, and he looks scared. A low whimper escapes his throat as if he is mentally tussling with the conundrum our father has posed.

"Do it. Save yourself, my friend." Andrei pushes his forehead against the gun barrel.

I'm praying and hoping Sasha doesn't pull the trigger. If he does, I'll lose them both. Their bond is so strong. Sasha will never forgive himself.

"No!" Sasha yells, headbutting my father, causing the gun to fly across the floor.

I scramble to get to it when Adam grabs my leg, tripping me.

"Come here, princess," he says and laughs, holding my ankle with his big hand.

I might be a princess, but I'm no ordinary one. I'm not a captive in a tower waiting for my prince to save me. I'm a mafia princess. I kick him with all my force, breaking his nose. He lets go of my ankle, bringing his hands to his face as copious blood trickles down between his trembling fingers.

When he releases me, my body quickly slides to the floor. I didn't think before acting, and now I stand here with a gun secured in my hand, holding it up to my father.

I look around and see that every enemy in the warehouse now has their firearms pointed at me. The weight of the gun feels heavy in my grasp.

Standing in front of me is a man I've known my entire life, a man I used to love once upon a time. But not recently, not for a long time.

My father signals for the men to lower their weapons, leaving this fight between me and him. "Sweetie, put the gun down." His hands raise, signaling for me to hand him the weapon.

A thumping sound is coming from my chest, filling my ears. Its blood flow is the only thing audible in this heightened tension. I grew up around guns but never held one before today, never imagining any need to.

He notices my hesitation and jumps forward.

"Stay back, or I'll shoot you." My grip grows tighter.

"You're not a killer," he says and steps forward with certainty in his stride.

"You don't know me!" I yell. He's never taken the time to get to know the girl I was, the woman I've become. He knows me less now than he ever has.

"Maybe I didn't always show you my love, but that doesn't mean it wasn't there." He takes another step forward.

"You hate me. You always have. I'd be a fool to think a man like you would ever have loved me." My vision blurs from the cascading tears.

He takes another step towards me. His eyes keep darting to my shaking hands.

"Look, it's time for you to stop acting like a child and hand me the gun." He takes two steps forward this time. He's not too far from me.

"I will shoot." I move closer to him.

"No, you won't. So, hand me the fucking gun, now!" His face turns sinister, and he starts to march toward me.

"I said I'll shoot!" I yell louder, but the man in front of me doesn't believe me, thinking I'm weak and nothing.

As I said, he doesn't know me. I'm Cora Belov. I grew up in the Russian Mafia, the Coalition, the Bratva. I may not be one of the men in power, but they've underestimated me.

He now stands close enough that the gun barrel is centimeters from his face, yet even with it pointed at him, his ruthless demeanor and demonic laugh overshadow me. His look says *you would never dare, you utter waste of space!*

"You slut!" He raises his hand to strike me. I see it coming, outstretched and flattened as if in slow motion, the world affording me time to obliterate him before the palm can contact my skin.

My hands still shake as I pull the trigger. The shot fires off, and my arm recoils with force, the sound muffled as the bullet penetrates the center of his forehead. In an instant, he is pushed back, brains and blood spraying from the gaping hole at the back of his head. Time freezes, giving me a satisfying view of that hideous man as he drops.

The gun tumbles from my hands, and I let out a cry, now aware of the enormity of it all and of what I have done. I stoop, trying to wipe the blood off his chest, but there's too much red. Holding my hands in the air, I see those red stains, how they are spreading and seeping.

With a harrowing breath, I wail. My ears pick up the most horrible, visceral shriek like the agonies of a dying animal. I realize that the sound is me. I'm rendered frozen to the spot, unable to move. *I've killed someone. I killed my own father!*

The building shakes, and there's a loud bang. Screaming, I crouch like a baby, covering my ears with a tight palm over each. Gunfire ricochets all around me, and I'm so scared. Suddenly, a familiar arm wraps around me, grabbing me and pulling me into his chest.

"I got you," Andrei whispers in my ear. It brings me some comfort, but still, I've just killed my father. Tucking my head into my beloved Andrei's body, the sobs come harder.

I've started a war, and now my future husband and twin brother must end it.

Chapter Twenty-Six

ANDREI

When I hear the explosion, I know my father has arrived. When the noise distracts the men, Sasha and I use our training to fight them until the time comes when Sasha can untie me. With my wrists freed, I immediately run to the girl crouched on the ground, screaming.

Dmitri covers us, aiming his gun at the enemy. I carry Cora to the corner of the warehouse. "Watch her," I order my brother.

I was completely shocked when she fired the gun. Murdering someone, especially her father, would have been unimaginable. I can only imagine how scared she was for her to shoot someone, especially that close in range.

Leaving Cora secure with my brother, I can now turn my attention to someone I plan to kill. *Boris!* This motherfucker grew up around the Coalition and is a few years older than us. He knew better than to touch a future Brigadiers wife.

Even if he had killed me, my father and brothers would have searched the world looking for her, burning everyone and everything in their path.

Ducking and moving around the warehouse, I turn every corner looking for him, but he's nowhere to be found. With my hands gripping my gun firmly, I walk outside in time to see him jumping into a vehicle and speeding off. Firing a few shots, the bullets hit the car with minimal damage, letting him get away. *Coward!*

It doesn't take long before the warehouse becomes quiet. When you're a Brigadier, an underground army is at your disposal. My father came with the Coalition Army, led by my brother, Nikolai. The Belov soldiers have all been killed. When you threaten the future Brigadier, there are no chances of you staying alive.

"Cora." I walk to her, arms open to bring her closer. But she pulls away from me. She's never done that before, and it causes physical pain in my chest.

"Sasha!" She wraps her arms around him, and he squeezes her firmly. "I'm so sorry. I—" He puts his finger on her soft lips, quieting her. There's no reason for her to explain herself. Her actions are warranted.

My father pulls me into a long hug. This was the first time my life was in danger without backup, and he must have felt petrified.

It's a feeling we shared when I realized Cora's life was in trouble. But this is the world we grew up in, and this won't be the last time our lives are threatened.

My father wraps his arm around Sasha's shoulder. "We'll take care of your mother. She'll be in Russia by tomorrow night."

Our lives are about to change. Cora and Sasha have lost their father, though whether either of them comprehends it as a loss remains to be seen. Cora will be filled with remorse and self-reproach for her slaying of the brute.

The guy standing next to me looks saddened, too. My best friend was faced with a choice between his father and me, and he chose me. I hope he doesn't regret his decision.

"What do we do now?" Sasha asks my father.

For both of them, my dad has always been the father Mr. Belov never cared to be. Even if Cora didn't know it, my father always cared for everything she wanted or needed. She is as much a Savin as Sasha is.

"You're my son, Sasha. You'll go home with us." My father embraces him in a hold. "You too," my father tells Cora, placing his hand on the small of her back, patting her gently, offering her what little comfort he can. It is a minuscule gesture, but he means well.

Cora gives him a slight smile before pulling away. "I'm not going back to New York. I'm going to spend the summer in London." She looks directly at me, insisting, "Do not try to stop me, Andrei. I need to do this for me."

"Cora, no. It's not safe. You need to be in New York by my side."

Her cold eyes move away from mine. Is the hateful look she's giving directed toward me? Or is it her feeling about the day? She doesn't want to be with me right now, and the thought of not having her near me for a few months hurts a surprising amount.

Without another word, she turns and walks away. My brother Nikolai grabs her arm and guides her to a vehicle while I stand back, watching her lean her head on his shoulder as they exit. They've had a kindred friendship since they were young, and I can trust Nikolai to keep her safe. But still, I am the one who is supposed to look after her.

No, I can't let her leave. I walk toward her purposefully, needing to stop her. But I'm stopped when my father reaches out, grabbing me.

"If you love her, the best thing you can do is let her breathe," my father tells me. "Sometimes, people need space."

That's not the advice I want to hear from him right now. But, deep down, I know he's right. Cora went through a traumatic experience today, and she will need time to internalize it. For once, I need to put her before my own selfish needs.

"What do we do now?" I ask him.

"A war was started today. We'll head back to New York and find Boris. Anyone associated with today's attacks will be eliminated." Sasha stands next to my father, nodding in agreement.

"What about these two?" Dmitri interjects, pointing at Adam and Nicole.

"I'll leave them to you," I tell Sasha.

Laughing, he and Dmitri escort them out of the building. The two of them won't be showing up on campus next semester.

"Let's head home. We have a war to finish!" I tell my dad, ready to return to New York and finish a war started today.

And I hope that at the end of summer, Cora will choose to return to me.

Chapter Twenty-Seven

ANDREI

SOPHOMORE YEAR

The man's body hangs from ropes in the alleyway, slightly swaying there, as the nauseating stench of his decaying flesh fills the air, reminiscent of leather slowly being tanned over a flame.

My lips press together, determined to keep the thick, rich stench from touching my taste buds. My breathing almost stops at the moment I see him swaying there.

That man is Boris, the last of the despised Belov men to meet his end.

There is no one left of the Belov crime family except for Sasha, Cora, and their mother.

I pause just before getting into the vehicle, stealing a glance at my friend who walks silently beside me.

His eyes appear saddened, not for the scum burning before us both, but because this hideous act announces the very end of his family's legacy.

"Sasha." My voice is shaky, an annoying tremor refusing to be suppressed.

Holstering his gun behind his back, Sasha's eyes squint at the dark sky. "So, it's over," he says resignedly, yet a sigh of relief leaves him before he enters the SUV.

Once inside, a look of concern burns on my face. "I'm sorry…"

He cuts me off, raising a flat palm. *"Sorry?* My father did this to our family. You only did what needed to be done to protect Cora."

I turn my head away from him. Sasha and Cora look so much alike, rendering this summer hellishly painful. Working alongside her twin is a challenge. He's a constant reminder of Cora, who I've lost and miss dearly.

"Hey, I miss her too," he whispers, patting my knee.

As the future Brigadier, I'm forbidden to show weakness to my men, to the Coalition, or even to Sasha, my friend. He knows how much I've been missing her this summer without me having to say a word. I gaze out the window to hide the tear that insists on falling.

I find my father with the Pakhan and Valentin on the terrace of the penthouse, atop *El Grande*, an exclusive high-rise operated by the Coalition in New York. Only the Coalition's members may reside there, and very few ever visit the Pakhan in his exclusive home.

I grew up visiting him anytime according to my wishes. The Pakhan is my mother's brother and this relationship offered me a rite of passage. My family lives on the fifty-sixth floor, directly beneath him.

My uncle, father, and godfather all grew up together. Our three families created the Coalition. Now, the three men sitting before me share a tight bond that only strengthens our positions in the underground world. Their friendship is solid and built on trust, a quality almost impossible to find in the world of organized crime.

Standing before the men, arms behind my back, I wait rigidly until they acknowledge me.

"Andrei," Uncle calls me forward, gesturing for me to join them. And I do.

Valentin hands me a glass of liquor and a cigar from the box, something to savor, a time for bonding.

There's probably more learning on its way, I sense, since 'learning' often takes place over cigars and vodka. Over the years, so much knowledge about this business has come my way from these three men. Their discussions, debates, and stories are always lessons, imparting the knowledge I need to become the next Brigadier.

My respect for them has deepened, and I look up to each of them in different ways for the vital roles they've played in my life, shaping me into the man I am today.

But this summer has been tough.

"Eliminate the Belov legacy," they said. At that moment, my thoughts ran wild. *That's my best friend and my future wife's family and legacy. For God's sake, don't make me!*

But now, the ugly deed was done. A task struck off the 'to-do' list.

"It's over?" my father asks in a nonchalant tone as if asking about the end of a movie.

"Yes, Brigadier." My right eye flickers in an uneasy tic. "It is over."

Even though I long for this ordeal to end, thoughts of the conclusion fill me with dread, knowing that's when the inevitable discussion with my father will take place.

"And Sasha?" he inquires. My father has been worrying about Sasha all summer, loving him like a son. With poor Sasha's father dying, my father frets that now, Sasha could change his loyalties. After all, we have stolen his family's legacy and robbed him of the little he had.

But it won't happen. Sasha has my trust. And why wouldn't he? He's been by my side through every assignment. We faced it all together, even the toughest moments.

"He did what had to be done." My arm extends, firmly placing the glass on the table next to me, tired of discussing this godforsaken topic. The glass clattering on the tabletop conveys it.

"What's on your mind, Andrei?" Valentin interjects, sensing my dread of talking to my father.

"Sasha and I are headed back to Seattle in the morning." With that, my guts set off roiling and churning.

Father slams his fist on the table, a too-predictable reaction. "Your place is here in New York with us." He doesn't even raise his voice; the words alone send chills down my spine.

My eyes move to the Pakhan and Valentin, hoping they will provide me some backup. They give me none, agreeing with my father.

"My place is with Cora. I was a good son this summer. Did everything you asked. But now it's time for me to be a good future husband and be there for her when she returns home." I've already made up my mind. I stand to end the discussion.

"Brigadiers don't put women before business," he states as he approaches me. Before I know it, I'm pushed against the wall with his hand around my throat.

"That's your way, Dad," I gasp out, struggling to breathe. The more I try to wriggle from his grasp, the tighter he grips my neck.

My father doesn't put his hands on his sons often, mainly because we always do what he asks. I was prepared for the fallout but won't change my mind.

Realizing he's lost control of himself, he releases me. I'm disappointing him, something I've tried my whole life to avoid.

"Let the boy go back to Seattle," my uncle interjects.

My father may disagree, but he won't defy the Pakhan.

"You keep saying you want to do things differently when you become Brigadier. Then, I guess we will wait and see what that is. We trust your judgment, nephew. I have no doubt you will not disappoint us." My uncle wraps his arms around me.

"Thank you, Pakhan." I bow down and kiss the ring on his hand, a sign of respect.

Valentin wraps me in a hug, bidding farewell to me.

I hesitate to leave, not wanting to depart New York with my father's disapproval. Silently, he stands there puffing on his cigar, looking over the terrace at the city's bright night sky.

"Dad." I stand beside him, taking in the view.

He wraps his arms around my neck, embracing me in his tight hold. "I love you, Son," he says in a low tone, ending our moment with a kiss on my cheek.

"I love you too, Dad." It's time for me to leave.

The three men I've admired my entire life go back to smoking and drinking as I walk back inside. Before leaving, I look back at them for a moment.

I hope that one day I can measure up to them.

Chapter Twenty-Eight

CORA

London is one of the oldest of the world's great cities and home to a veritable plethora of landmarks. While I enjoyed my writing classes during the week, I saved the weekends for exploring from Big Ben to the Borough Market. Its beautiful green parks are perfect for reading and thinking.

I needed time to myself. What I did to my father was a fatal mistake that ended my family. I have barely spoken to my mom since his death. Even though she loves me, I can hear the heartbreak of his loss in her voice every time we talk. Not only did she lose her husband, but she was also forced to leave her home in New York and return to Russia for her safety.

My brother and future husband made New York City rain in crimson blood, killing every person who was in support of my father. The only remains of the Belov family are us Belov twins. And the only person to blame for all of this is my father. Raised in the Coalition, he knew starting a war against the Savins would end in his death. Only an arrogant fucker would ever think he could have won against Mr. Savin and Andrei. But my father was always that, an arrogant fucker if ever there was one.

Most of the time since removing myself from the scene, I have been leaving my phone silent to avoid being distracted by their calls and messages, needing to work through my guilt and feelings alone. But, at night, when I lie in bed alone and lonely, I listen to his voicemails and cry. Being away from Andrei for the summer has broken my heart, and I've missed him deeply.

I scanned my surroundings, watching and waiting, expecting to find the Bratva watching me. But I never found them. It seems that, at last, Andrei has respected my feelings and understood the need to be away from the life we all grew up in.

Each day has been a different experience for me. Sometimes, I have felt furious at my father as I played out the scene repeatedly. What would have happened if I hadn't shot him? Then the thought scares me because what if I had not taken the shot, and what if, because of that, he'd managed to kill Andrei?

The nightmares came days after I pulled the trigger, and they have been returning every night without fail. The lack of sleep has, however, brought something positive, bringing with it the motivation and time to pour my soul into my book. *I finished writing my first story!*

Arriving in Seattle, the loudest rainfall greets me, as if the city knows what I did before I left her and is drowning out the noise for me. Each drop offers the calmness I longed for in London.

After the mess with Nicole and Adam, the boys are reluctant to let me live on campus again. But I refuse to live with them, still needing my space. After some arguing, Andrei has agreed to let me move next door to them. This arrangement allows me to keep my privacy while surrounded by security operatives.

The vehicle pulls up to my new apartment and with the release of my deep breath, I step out of the vehicle.

Entering my apartment, I'm reminded of who I am and who I'm expected to be. As a future Brigadier's wife, living in luxury is part of the deal. I've never cared for it, but appearances are important in the underground world. So, it's no surprise that my new apartment is decorated with lavish furniture. I'm sure Mrs. Savin helped. It has her style all over it.

I hear the boys entering my apartment, and when I look back at the door, I find my brother Sasha standing there, looking more like my father than ever before. My only response is a rush of tears.

Chapter Twenty-Nine

SASHA

I hide my anger toward her, not wanting to be hurtful. Cora doesn't deserve that.

As much as she has needed her space this summer, I have needed her! She's my twin sister. We've always been close, and even when she thought I wanted to be with the Savins more than her, it wasn't true. My loyalty is to Andrei. He's my future Brigadier and best friend, but I would never let anyone hurt Cora. But I had failed her. In the end, it was she who saved us, and she did it by killing our father.

I want nothing but to drop to my knees and beg her for forgiveness, acknowledging that all that has happened to her was my fault. I had known my father had been hurting her, but I had cowardly turned the other way, instead choosing to spend more time with Andrei and the Savin family to avoid the situation. Now, my sister has to carry a burden with her for the rest of her life.

Andrei and I were raised to be killers. As men of the Coalition, we kill to avoid being killed, weapons and violence coming along with our chosen life of organized crime. But that's not the life Cora was supposed to experience. She's a future Brigadier's wife. And as such, she's instead supposed to get the privileges that come with it- money, power, reputation, and children.

Women of this life aren't supposed to kill men, especially their fathers. So, I did this to her, and I will never forgive myself for allowing it to happen. For the rest of my life, I vow to protect my sister no matter the cost, even if it means turning against Andrei.

I see the guilt in her eyes, and when she begins to cry, I run to her, pulling her into my arms. There are no words to say. She needs to feel my arms around her.

She tries to pull away from me, but we're enveloped in a stronghold as two more arms wrap around us. This ordeal is something we've faced together-the three of us. It's always been Andrei and the twins. We're family, and we'll always have each other.

We stand in silence while we comfort each other. From this day forward, we have a stronger bond that will never break.

"I love you guys," I whisper, then pull them into a deeper hold.

I love you both more than you'll ever know.

Chapter Thirty

ANDREI

I enjoy listening to her recounting her summer, especially her writing classes, with excitement in her eyes. But I already know all this.

Cora wanted space this summer, and after the hellish ordeal of having to kill her own father, she deserved it. But I couldn't have my future wife running around London freely, not when we were raging a war against the Belovs, her family. So, I paid for a private security detail to follow her every day, each day a different man so that she wouldn't get suspicious.

Cora knows our life, having been trained to watch her surroundings. The company I paid for managed to get a student into her classes, someone she speaks of now. I hid this from Sasha as well. As much as she needed space, so did Sasha. Each morning, I received a brief on what she had done the day before, with pictures. I can't deny that seeing her every day helped fill my void for her a little, as I would sit and look at her photos for too long.

"Classes start tomorrow," I venture, telling her something she already knows. "Since you no longer have to take business classes, we won't be in the same courses this semester."

A faint smile forms on her face. I knew Cora would be excited about her new schedule she got to pick herself.

"Michael will be accompanying you to all your classes."

She acknowledges with a nod. I hope Cora has learned her lesson about sneaking out and ditching her security detail. Her stunt last semester could have cost her life.

The room becomes smaller as I stare at her, standing too close to her.

"Good night, Cora." Reaching down, I press my lips against hers. She doesn't open her mouth, not letting me in, but I feel her slight press against my lips in return. Her slightest reaction gives me hope that she still loves me.

I haven't been able to sleep in months, each night turning in my bed, thinking of that night Cora was made into one of us, a killer. I failed to protect her, and she paid the price, paying with bloody nightmares she'll have to live with daily. I find myself staring at the rain outside my window. The rainfall here in Seattle offers a calmness that is different from New York.

My ears perk up, hearing the front door open. Security knows better than to come in at night.

Soft footsteps pad across the condo and stop short at my door.

I stretch my fingers under my pillow and place them around the gun trigger. The doorknob jiggles before the door creaks open. My back still faces the door, but regardless, I know exactly where the person is, their shallow breathing pervading the air as they sneak into my room. Whoever it is slowly touches my bed, making the mattress sag as they climb onto it. I grip the gun tighter, about to pull it on my visitor.

And that is when her soft skin touches my arm. *Cora.*

Pulling the covers back, she slides her petite body against mine, her hardened nipples pressing on my back. When she drapes her arm around my chest, I place the safety back on my weapon.

Our fingers tangle as I hold her hand against my chest, by my heart. Her breaths on my neck melt me. *She still loves me!* Finally, I can breathe again.

My head spins around to meet hers, her beautiful eyes looking into mine, her parted lips irresistible. Unexpectedly, she makes the first move. Her kiss fills me with emotion.

She tangles her fingers in my hair, playing with it. Reaching over, I put my hand around her neck, pulling her into me. A slight purr escapes her mouth. Pushing me against the bed, she glides down my stomach, kissing me softly along her way down my waist. She pulls my boxers down slowly, showcasing my erection.

I haven't touched another woman since my last time with Cora. She bops her head down, taking my cock into her mouth whole. A deep growl escapes me. Her blowjob is way better than my imagination and jerking off I did all summer.

Slipping my cock out of her mouth, she moves her tongue up and down my shaft until she places my balls into her mouth, sucking them one at a time.

Stroking my cock with one hand, I try to keep from coming. My moans tell her I'm close.

Slowly, she takes off her nightgown, slipping her wet pussy around my cock. Her hips move up and down, offering a visual delight to see her tits bounce as she's working up to an orgasm. She's mine to control, and although she's enjoying the ride, I tightly grip both of her tits. She lets out a painful cry when I do so but rides my cock even harder.

Watching Cora riding out her pleasure is personal to me. Knowing I'm the only man who will ever make her feel this way makes me love her more. There's no performance here, no exaggerated movements, none of the sounds you would find in porn. Just the deep intimacy between me and my future wife.

An indescribable connection exists between us, one that's been there since the moment we met. I knew I loved her when I was just five years old. When people speak of true love, they tell our story—Cora's and mine. Our love is a unique and passionate bond that ties us together in a way that feels almost exceptional.

Cora begins to lose control, bucking on my cock wildly as my finger circles her clit. "Come for me, Kitten," I tell her. The quiet room fills with her screams as she shatters on my cock. Her wet juices drip down my waist and thigh. It feels too good, and it's been too long since I've felt her. Now it's time for me to finish.

Grabbing her hips, I pull her down on me harder. Thrusting my hips into her tiny body, I fill her with my hot cum. The relief brings me a calmness I've needed these past months, not knowing if I would ever get to make love to her again.

Fuck, Cora makes me feel invincible!

I roll over to hold her against me while we fall asleep, but she moves my arm from her chest. As she quietly leaves my bed, I call out to her, "Stay."

Without a response, she walks out of my room, and minutes later, I hear the front door shut. I let out a deep breath and close my eyes.

The next morning, I woke to find myself alone, questioning if her earlier visit was just a dream.

Inadvertently, I stretch my arms out and touch something soft. Lifting it, my heartbeat skips again, seeing she's left her nightgown on the bed. The thought that I could still win her back brings a faint smile to me.

I'm now ready for the first day of a new semester.

Chapter Thirty-One

CORA

"This is a page-turner," Dr. Cullen says as he taps his pointer finger on the cover. Before leaving London, I sent my professor a copy of the manuscript I had finished over the summer.

I used this accomplishment to avoid missing Andrei, but it didn't work. Seeing him the other night made me crave him again. When the boys left, leaving me to my thoughts, I could only think about how handsome he looked in his black suit. *Gosh, I missed him!*

When my fingers between my legs weren't enough to satisfy my cravings, I found myself gravitating to his bedroom, longing for Andrei's touch, his moans, his cum inside me.

"It's still somewhat choppy, so you'll need to edit," Dr. Cullen comments, cutting into my thoughts. "Or you can have a good editor look at it." Slipping a business card across his desk, I take it to find he's given me the contact for a book editor.

This is the first excitement I've felt in a long time. "You think it's really worth publishing?"

"Absolutely! A story about true love and the violent things the two of them have to do to be together; the readers will love it! The scene about her killing her own father to save him, I could almost imagine myself there, experiencing it. How did you produce the idea for the plot?"

"An idea came up in my head. That's why it's called fiction. We get to just make the story up," I answer.

He laughs, "I suppose I asked for that."

But this story is largely based on my life. When readers visualize it, they will have no idea there was no imagination on the author's part and that it is essentially non-fiction. I've lived it and continue living it daily.

Dr. Cullen is my academic advisor now that I don't have to attend business courses.

The first week of the semester has been full of writing classes, and it's hard to imagine a better way to start my sophomore year. After a few minutes of additional advice from my new advisor, I head out of his office to start the weekend but only make it a few steps down the hallway before running into the devil himself.

"Hello, Kitten," Andrei says as he hands me a cup of coffee before pecking my cheek with his soft lips.

"What's the occasion?" I ask him as we start leaving campus.

"I don't need a reason to see my future wife," he answers loud enough that the girls walking by can hear him. I slightly turn my head to hide myself from their scowls.

At the end of the sidewalk, Sasha waits for us with the car. "Where are we going?" I ask Andrei.

With a big grin, he doesn't answer as he opens the door for me to get in.

Seattle is a breathtaking city. During my first semester, I often visited it during the weekend to explore. It is surrounded by beautiful mountain peaks and the calm Pacific Ocean.

We stop inland where the community gathers for a street fair. As I step onto the sidewalk, the Russian language surrounds me, and it feels like I'm home. "Andrei," I kiss him on the cheek as he takes my hand, walking through the street together.

Andrei and Sasha must be busy working as we are greeted by business community men. Being the largest and most successful Bratva worldwide, high-ranking Coalition members are well known throughout our community. I know all too well the politics of organized crime. And I can already guess that as much as Andrei wanted to share the feeling of home with me, a business meeting is planned for this visit.

A smell passes my nose, and my stomach rumbles with excitement. "Blini!" I grip Andrei's hand and pull him into the bakery, a slice of heaven in this little corner shop. Blini is a Russian crepe and one of my favorite things to eat when I visit Russia.

The cute older couple behind the counter serves me a piece. I'm devouring its deliciousness before Andrei can pull out his wallet. He hands the older gentleman a hundred-dollar bill when he declines his payment. This is how the community shows its respect. Andrei politely says thank you and places the bill in their tip jar.

A tall blond man walks into the bakery, and Andrei has Michael escort me back to the street before the men disappear behind closed doors. *I called it. It's business as usual!*

Little girls take the stage and perform their ballet routine, and for the first time, I imagine having a daughter of our own. He has vowed he would never promise our daughter in a business exchange, chattels to be sold off. I'm pretty lucky, in fact, to have been promised to my true love while other women were taken from their homes to live with monsters.

I get upset thinking about it. Andrei has made promises of a new Coalition one day, a vision in which I've heard his brothers support him. And, if anyone can do it, it's the Savin brothers. I need to see where I can fit into this new world, not on the sidelines but as a contributor.

After a long night in 'our' community, we arrive home just in time for my body to start fading from the rush of the earlier excitement and my stomach full of food.

Standing in front of my door, Andrei pulls me into him. "Spend the night with me?" he asks.

"I'm not ready to return to how we were before the summer. But today was a start." I extend myself and kiss him. When his lips open slightly, my tongue reacts and begins to wrestle his. Our kiss is long and passionate.

I break our kiss and close my apartment door when his hand slams against it. I grip the handle harder, pushing it shut, but he's too strong for me. "Andrei!" I cry out as the door flings open.

Andrei backs me against the wall, his eyes no longer angelic but black like the dark night outside. "You belong to me, Cora. Remember that."

"Get off me," I scream, pushing his chest, but his body comes closer to mine.

His mouth is so close to me, and his breath is hot on my neck. "Get off me," I whisper, my arms no longer pushing against his muscled frame. My fingers are now crawling up his neck until they begin to twirl his hair.

"Get off me," I purr when his lips touch mine. With our bodies pressed together, our arms become tangled as we stand at the door in a fury of kisses.

He halts suddenly, stepping back, and before I can process what's happening, my door slams shut in my face. I stand there, trying to catch my breath, my head spinning from the whirlwind of emotions. With a deep sigh, I remind myself that things have changed. I'm broken now, and it's not Andrei's job to put me back together.

Chapter Thirty-Two

ANDREI

"Good evening, Cora." My father pulls her into a tight hug. Since she found out she's a future Savin, my family has embraced her more than before to make her feel a part of our family. It's a kind sentiment from one of the most feared men in the world.

Cora takes her seat next to me. We all have an assigned place at the table. In the Savin family, your seating is based on family rank, which is very traditional but common in our world. My father sits at the head of the table with my mother directly across from him. As the eldest son, I sit to my father's right, my fiancée beside me. My four brothers are also assigned seats at the table based on age. Since they aren't here tonight, Sasha sits next to the Brigadier.

The restaurant is one of the finest in Seattle and extremely busy on a Saturday night. Our table is in a private room at the back of the restaurant. Security stands at the door and more outside the building. My father always travels with an entourage.

"What brings you both to Seattle," Cora asks my parents. *Yes, why is my father here?*

He was very vague on the phone about their reasons for visiting. Most college kids would love a visit from their parents. As much as I enjoy seeing them, Brigadiers don't have the time to visit their college sons across the country unless there's some specific reason. I am still waiting to hear what that specific reason might be.

"Business." My father places a folder on the table next to his wine glass. Then he pauses, saying, "Cora, this envelope belongs to you." Yet he hands the envelope to me instead of her.

After reading its contents, I give Cora a cautious look before passing the envelope over to her.

"What is this?" she asks.

My father speaks out. "Your father's estate left half of the family business to you. The other half, of course, to Sasha." He hands Sasha an envelope as well.

The numbers on the papers equate to millions of dollars. A tightness grips my chest, seeing the only thing this paperwork brings her is more pain and the memory of her father.

After placing the papers back in the envelope, she pushes it in front of me. "I don't want it."

Cora is my future wife, and with my family's wealth exceeding a billion dollars, she won't need anything from him.

"We don't know anything about running businesses," Sasha tells my dad and hands me his envelope as well.

"Doesn't my share have to go to Andrei anyway?" she asks my dad. I glance over at him as he nods. That was the agreement. In actuality, she only owns her share until our wedding day.

"Mr. Savin, I have a proposition," Cora says, surprising all of us. It's unlike her to make a deal with my dad.

His eyebrow raises in response, intrigued by what Cora could possibly ask of him. I know I am.

The waiter cuts in and serves our meal, easing some tension around the table.

"I'll sign over my estate right now if you grant me one favor." I watch Sasha move in his seat. He's nervous, and I don't think he knows what Cora wants from my father.

"Can you please let my mother return to New York?" Her voice cracks.

I admit it's unfair that their mother has suffered the loss of her husband and has been forced to move from her home. This is a fair ask from Cora. Their mother is the only family they have left.

My father doesn't respond. I see Cora's fingers tremble subtly as she sips her water. This is how my father rules, with fear. But it's not fair for him to do this to her, the closest person he's ever had to a daughter.

So, for the first time, I tap my father's foot with mine. When he looks at me, I quickly nod to approve her request.

"I'll have my plane pick her up. She'll be under the Savin protection when she returns." She gives him a huge smile, thanking him. This is the first time since she's returned that I've seen a glimmer of hope in her eyes. I hope this is a step forward in her healing process.

None of us have touched our food. We don't dare start eating until my father begins his meal, so when he picks up his fork and places a piece of steak in his mouth, we follow and start our family dinner.

We may have fooled my parents tonight, but make no mistake, we're not the happy couple we're trying to portray to my parents, more specifically, my mother. We're co-existing every day together, barely saying more than a short and casual conversation. Cora's hurt, and for the first time in my life, I don't know what to do about it. I'm the future leader of this family and can't even fix my own girlfriend.

After dessert, my father sends Cora and my mother to visit the boutique next door. "I think I saw a few pretty dresses when we walked by. You ladies should pick out one for yourselves before they close," he says as he hands my mother his credit card.

When only the men are left at the table, my father pauses slowly sipping his coffee, deep in thought. "A new threat is brewing."

"Do we know who this enemy is?" I ask him.

"No, but it's inside the Coalition." *Coalition men!*

I don't need to ask why. The things we did this summer, killing off anyone associated with Sasha's father, didn't sit well with everyone.

"I have an idea to make the Savins the most powerful family in the Bratva." My father fills in the details for Sasha and me.

I'm a threat to the older members of the Bratva, positioning myself as one of the most influential emerging leaders in organized crime. Not only do I have a future Brigadier title, but my innovative methods for generating revenue also intimidate the older leaders. They're used to selling women and drugs to make money, not leveraging technology innovation to see us earn more than ever, yet inputting only half the risks and the work.

In the end, during my reign, the men who support my plans will make more wealth than they can imagine. Those who are reluctant will cease to exist.

A new era is coming in organized crime, and I plan to lead it.

Chapter Thirty-Three

CORA

Holding the door open, I look at my options for far too long. *Sauvignon Blanc it is!* After uncorking the bottle, I take a swig before pouring it into the glass.

Nerves churned in my stomach as I approached Mr. Savin, dreading the conversation about whether my mom could return to New York. I expected him to refuse, but to my surprise, not only would she be coming back, but she'd also be under the protection of the Savin family. This meant no Bratva enemies would dare touch her as retribution for my father's sins. I hope moving back home will give her a little comfort as she works through her grief. My father may have been an evil man, but he was her husband, and she loved him.

Taking this moment to celebrate, I put on music and dance around the room. In this life and my role, people are always watching, so the stress from the pressure they exert on me can become overwhelming. It feels good to be alone, free from judging eyes. I am no longer thinking of before summer, the burdens of being a Brigadier's wife, or my next steps with my book. It's just me, dancing until I grow lightheaded.

Pouring the last of the bottle into my glass, I stumble enough to spill some of its liquid on my dress. *"Crap!"* I slip my dress over my head and walk into the bedroom where my silhouette catches my eye in the ceiling-to-wall mirror. Stopping in front of it, I gaze at myself. Nothing about me is exotic.

No big boobs, no big ass. I also don't work out often, softening my muscles. But I'm still happy in my own skin. My thin body doesn't need to be perfect for Andrei to love touching it.

I watch myself as my hips sway to the music, my finger slightly touching my breast. This past summer, nightly, I would think of Andrei, sliding my fingers in and out of me, imagining his cock inside of me until I would explode and moan his name. I had missed him so much!

The sound of my phone pulls me out of my thoughts. Andrei has sent me a text. *Goodnight. You looked beautiful tonight.* Too bad he can't see me now.

Deciding to do something I've never done before, I snap a picture of my naked body with the tip of my finger pulling down my lower lip. Pausing before I hit send, I wonder … will he find it trashy? But I look beautiful and want him to see me. Plus, I would love to be the last thing he thinks about in bed tonight, so my fingertip hits the send button before there's time to change my mind.

I wait, looking down at my phone. He appears to be responding, but the dots showing he is replying suddenly cease. He has disappeared. A knot forms in my stomach not knowing his thoughts, and I find myself quickly disappointed. *What was I thinking?*

Deciding it's time to head to bed and regain some of my dignity tomorrow, I down the last of my wine and rinse the glass. Giving myself one last glance in the mirror, I think *I look good! It's his loss.*

Knuckles hit against my door. Before I can answer it, the knob turns, and the door swings open. Standing before me is a shirtless Andrei with a bulge pressing against his gray pants.

"Thought you were headed to bed?"

"I can leave if that's what you want," he replies, taking a few steps forward.

Realizing I've been staring at his waist area way too long, I find the biggest smirk on his face.

Feeling self-conscious, my arms quickly cross to hide myself. He grabs them and pulls them behind me. "Why are you hiding? You wanted me to see you, didn't you? That's why you sent that text."

"I'm sorry, I was just ..." My lips are but a few inches from his.

"Feeling a little naughty?" He finishes my sentence. "Was that music I heard earlier?"

"Just dancing around," I reply, my face red from embarrassment.

"Let me see." He leaves me in the hallway alone and moves to the lounge chair. I follow him and find him sitting there, knees wide open.

The music still plays, and I stand in front of him, unsure what to do. "Dance," he commands.

Awkwardly, my hips begin swaying from side to side. I feel stupid, but I gaze at his face, and he's watching me and enjoying the show. Something about Andrei gives me confidence, so I move my hips more, adding a bounce to my ass. I turn around, my legs between his thighs and surprise myself when I bend completely, showing my asshole to him.

"Naughty girls get punished. Are you a naughty girl?" he asks me.

"Yes, Brigadier. I've been a naughty girl. I need to be punished."

This is a different side of Andrei, one I have yet to see. His face is more sinister, almost making me frightened of him. Then his eyes soften, a smile forming. *He's having fun with me.*

"Get on your knees, Cora," he commands me. I follow his orders, moving my mouth to his bulge that has risen, sticking out my tongue and licking him through the fabric of his sweatpants.

Pulling down his pants, I grab his cock with my hand, moving it up and down as his bulge enlarges. I spit on it before gliding my tongue from the tip to his balls. He opens my mouth wide with his finger and starts to shove his cock in me inch by inch.

With each thrust, his tip hits the back of my throat, making me gag as a reflex, but he doesn't stop. He thrusts hard, making me suck him entirely. I can barely breathe, trying to pull away to catch my breath, but he doesn't let me. His hands hold my head in place for a few more thrusts. With his hands, he jerks himself off and leaves me waiting patiently on my knees, mouth open. It doesn't take long before he comes. I take him whole again and suck him off as he squirts into my mouth. His penis pulsates, and I gladly swallow every last drop, licking my lips.

It's a far more intense mental and physical experience, and one of the rarest forms of control I have over Andrei, the future Brigadier, the man men fear. So, there is much pleasure in these experiences with Andrei, making him lose himself to me, like an award for a job well done.

Chapter Thirty-Four

ANDREI

I've been drowning in school and Cora that I've failed to achieve any work. A new threat is brewing. In our lives, there's always a threat, but taking out an entire family empire over a few months threatens all those in the Bratva. And now the men think the Savins are getting greedy for power. I just wanted to protect Cora.

I don't regret anything I did this summer. They hurt the one thing I love more than even my family. A lot of men in organized crime don't put their women on pedestals, marrying instead for convenience, as a business contract, or to birth and raise future heirs to their family fortune.

Even though my parents' marriage was arranged, I couldn't help but admire the way my father loved my mother. As a Bratva boss, he had the weight of the world on his shoulders, yet he still found time for the little gestures that spoke volumes- sending her flowers, kissing her on the cheek, or resting a reassuring hand on her lower back. She always responded with a smile and affection in her eyes. I knew the moment I was arranged to marry Cora that this was the kind of relationship I wanted with her.

But those little things aren't easy for a man like me. We are raised to be violent. I've learned to kill a man with an assortment of weapons and with my bare hands. With the same hands with which I come home and give Cora the softest touches, often forgetting to wash the blood off my fingers, quickly rubbing any stains on my pants before I taint her.

A violent life takes you to a dark place in your mind. Even if I don't want to hurt or kill someone, if it's an order, they're dead. And we kill showing no empathy or remorse.

This is why men of organized crime don't love. It's easier to turn off your feelings permanently than go back and forth like that. But I find a greater strength in my love for Cora and my family.

My desire to protect and provide for them allows me to look beyond the violence, revealing alternative ways to make the enemy suffer—methods that don't rely on physical harm.

Last summer, I found a tech kid in one of my classes. I offered to pay for his college tuition and to give him more money than any of these tech firms would in exchange for working in the Savin Corporation as a hacker. The older men of the Coalition can't grasp this new concept. But if you want to take down an enemy, start by bankrupting them. So much power lies there.

"Where have you been?" I ask Sasha when he stumbles into the apartment in the same clothes he wore last night.

"I spent the night with Amy," he replies, flopping onto the couch.

"The cheerleader with the big boobs?" He's always been a boobs and blondes guy. Whereas I've always been more attracted to more natural girls. In high school, I always looked for girls who reminded me of Cora, often fantasizing they were her.

Although my father trusts Sasha and loves him like a son, he's cautious right now since we killed his family. Even when a man's loyalties are to the Savins, losing a parent can change that. So, my father instructed me to keep an eye on him.

Sasha's phone rings, and he steps into his bedroom to take the call. I put down my coffee and lightly walk by his door, pressing my ear to it. Sasha's muffled voice is just about audible.

"It's almost time. No, believe me, Andrei doesn't suspect a thing."

The doorknob jiggles, and before I step away, Sasha stands there looking at me. "Want to grab lunch?" I ask him. Nodding, he begins to put on a fresh change of clothes. I narrowly escaped getting caught spying on him.

We pick a little café around campus where we'll dine. Growing up in New York, we've always dined at the best restaurants and had a personal chef to make food just as good at home. But here in Seattle, I've been enjoying all the little shops full of college kids. It's a distraction from home, and no one even knows the Savins here.

I hate to admit it, but it does feel good to be a regular college student, even for a small amount of time.

"You've been busy lately," I tell Sasha. He's been disappearing a lot this past month without a word, acting secretive and silent, kind of introspective. This is not the Sasha I know. Since we were kids, we have always stayed in contact with each other, knowing where the other is in case of an issue or emergency.

There were occasions in high school when I would sneak off without a word just to go spy on Cora in the library. I'd watch her sitting in the corner, reading books or typing away at her writing. Especially on bad days, it felt good just to see her.

But this is different. He's hiding something. I know him better than anyone, even his twin.

"I've been hanging out with the ladies. You told me to enjoy college." He doesn't look up at me. I've learned he avoids eye contact when he's not quite telling the truth. He can lie with the straightest face to others but not to me.

I sit quietly eating my sandwich.

A text message alert comes through, and Sasha immediately picks up his phone to read it, tapping his finger against the screen. A tiny droplet of water runs down his forehead. Wiping his face with his napkin, he says, "I've got to be somewhere." Grabbing his jacket, he excuses himself.

I wait a few minutes before following him to one of our stash houses, an apartment we set up in the city as a place to stay in case we needed it to hide, equipping it with cash and weapons. I conceal myself behind a large van, waiting for him. About half an hour later, Sasha emerges from the apartment carrying a black bag, recognizable as one of our cash bags. It's unlike him to take a significant amount of money somewhere without talking to me. What is he up to?

Jumping into a taxi, I follow him until we reach the industrial district of Seattle. My cab driver drops me off a block past where Sasha stands.

Cutting through the alley, I stop behind a dumpster, then come in clear view of Sasha talking to someone. But who is it? The man's back is turned to me. They shake hands, and Sasha hands him the bag. When the man turns to leave, I recognize him as the professor. Again, my inner voice can't help asking, *what is he doing?*

Last year, I started a new adventure with the professor, creating shell companies that currently make a load of money here in the Pacific Northwest, investing in natural resources. Business has been great, and I'm turning the kind of profit the leaders of the Coalition couldn't even imagine. So why is Sasha meeting him directly and making a payment to him, one I don't know about?

When the professor leaves, I call Sasha.

"What's up?" he asks at the other end of the line.

"Where are you?"

"Came back to Amy's place. She sent some nudes, and I couldn't help myself, so we're enjoying each other's company if you know what I mean." His chuckle cracks.

"Just wanted to know if you wanted to join Cora and me for dinner." This isn't the time for me to act suspiciously. If I want to know what Sasha's up to, I'll have to string him along.

We both hang up, and I watch him leave. Was my father right all along? Is Sasha upset about his family and creating a threat against the Savins? A tightness grips my chest, the realization settling in that the one person I thought I could trust might be lying to me.

The feeling of betrayal overcomes me, and my fingertips dial the number for my father.

Chapter Thirty-Five

CORA

"Thank you so much!" Hanging up the phone, I jump onto my bed. *Is my dream really coming true? Can I really be this happy?*

I've sent my manuscript to the editor of a start-up book publishing company here in Seattle. She thinks I have a great story and is starting the first round of edits. With some hard work over this semester, I could have it published by my junior year of college.

Being a future Savin means I don't need money or fame since I'll be part of New York's billionaire elite club. So, publishing this book is important to me because it's something that's mine, *just mine.*

Ever since I was a little girl, reading and writing have been my outlet, my imagination allowing me to escape the sadness I felt with my father, overcoming depressing thoughts. It has allowed me to connect deeply with myself and bring joy into my own life. Being an author is a dream, giving me the outlet to share my stories. Knowing other girls will read them helps me find inspiration and creativity to build a different world. If other girls feel anything like the way I did growing up, I want to be part of their escape and a small part of creating their own happiness.

"Are you ready?" Andrei walks into the room. Not realizing the time, I jump into his arms and kiss him. "You're really happy today. Is there a reason why?" he asks.

"Just excited to spend the day with you," I reply.

"So, where are we going?"

I have set up a surprise for him today. We've been in Seattle for over a year and haven't yet enjoyed the things the Pacific Northwest has to offer. I head over to my desk to grab the bags of clothing we'll need. I notice a copy of my manuscript on the top of paperwork in plain sight, and I shuffle around the desk to bury it underneath my laptop. I can't tell him about my book; he'll be angry. We don't talk about the things we've done or seen. My book could be seen as a threat to our way of life.

The two-hour drive is filled with conversation and laughter between us, and it's so nice to have him to myself with no distractions. When he asks about school and more about my summer, he is completely interested in me, totally immersed. I share everything about my life with him, except that I already wrote a book and plan to publish it.

I feel bad, but right now is not the time.

The staggering mountain is topped with thick snow. A cold front has embarked upon Seattle early this winter, forcing us to wear our waterproof fabric jackets two months earlier than expected. When my foot dips into the powdered snow, Andrei's arms wrap around me from behind. "Snowboarding?" he asks.

When we were young, I joined the Savin family on their winter vacations to Utah for the ski season. The boys would descend the slope at rapid speeds while I took my time freeriding, my leisurely pace allowing me to enjoy the beauty of the mountains and the quietness of my thoughts.

But what I loved most about those trips was my time with Andrei around the house. I would sit quietly in Mr. Savin's office, reading my book after a long day outside. The warmth radiating from the fireplace and the humming of the burning wood brought a homely feeling New York never gave me.

When the other boys were too preoccupied to notice, Andrei would sneak over with a blanket, asking what I was reading. Sometimes, he'd lean in close, peering over my shoulder as if he were eager to catch a glimpse of the pages. After he rejoined the guys, I'd snuggle into the fabric, inhaling his familiar scent that lingered on the blanket.

The natural pillow feeling of the powdered snow makes the day bearable. It's been a while since we've been on the mountainside, and I find my ass repeatedly hitting the ground. Even Andrei struggles to stay on two feet, and I watch him as he loses control and hits the ground beside a tree. Wanting to make sure he was not hurt, I put more pressure on my toes, turned my board, and head toward him.

I find him sitting on the powder overlooking the view.

"It's pretty out here," he says, looking up at me with a laugh.

"Are you okay?"

"Thank you for this." His hand slips into mine as I pull him back up on his feet. I'm immersed in his eyes without any outside thoughts. When his cold, cracked lips touch mine, I lose myself in him, and a soft moan escapes me. My middle tingles when Andrei's finger caresses the outside of my snow pants. "Andrei," I whisper with a giggle. "Someone might see us."

He ignores me, unbuttoning my pants and pulling my panties to the side. His long finger begins to rub my clit. I forget about the snowboarders passing us by. My only thoughts are how good he makes me feel.

A loud moan escapes me when he inserts his finger in me until the length of it is entirely in me. As he holds me closely, I rotate my hips, riding the wave movement of him moving in and out of me slowly until my middle clenches, sending a loud gasp echoing between the trees.

Just then, cold dust hits my face as a snowboarder comes too close to us, racing down the mountainside. When Andrei laughs, I lift my gaze to his. His eyes have softened.

Over the past months, I've seen the stress of dissolving the Belov family weighing on him. I wish I could tell him how proud I am of the man he is.

No other nineteen-year-old man could walk in his shoes. Only Andrei could handle being a college student, a businessman, and a Bratva leader. On top of that, he's been so attentive to me and my needs.

Maybe I've been selfish. I am allowed to mourn the loss of my father and the fact that I was the one who killed him. But I've also got to show Andrei the same support he's shown me. The things he's done these past months were for me, things he did because those men supported my father in hurting me.

Andrei cuts into the cold silence. "I wish Sasha could have come today. He would have enjoyed this." Sasha's always been the most adventurous of the three of us.

"I invited him, but he said he had work." I give him a curious look.

"Do you know what Sasha's been up to?" Ever since we were kids, Sasha has been Andrei's shadow. I have noticed him sneaking out lately but assumed it was for a hot girl. Is their friendship wavering after all this time?

"No." A lot has happened recently. Is my brother becoming disloyal to Andrei? I hope not. If I had to choose between my future husband or twin brother, I'm unsure which one I would support. The thought of having to choose pains me.

"Last one to the bottom buys dinner," Andrei proclaims and releases his grip, descending the hill. I lean forward, weaving down the mountain until I pass him on the last stretch.

Chapter Thirty-Six

ANDREI

My nose twitches, catching the faint fumes of sizzling bacon. Sasha can't cook, so I begin to wonder if my mom decided to surprise us with a visit. My eyes slowly open as the sun streaks through the blinds. The first thing I notice is Cora missing. Lately, she's been surprising me with consistent sleepovers, but she always sneaks out first thing in the morning.

As I enter the kitchen expecting my mom, I'm greeted with a loud cry of, "Fuck!"

Cora stands over the stove in a light gray pajama set which, despite not being at all revealing, fits so tightly around her petite body. The hot oil steams and pops in time to how my cock begins to twitch and dance.

Cora curses when the oil's spatter lands on her hand.

Positioning my body against hers, I grab the tongs and flip the bacon slices over before they burn. Like Savins, Cora grew up with a chef, so we weren't raised to be good cooks. Cora, however, has always been a great baker. She would spend hours in the kitchen baking various Russian desserts with our mothers.

"I wanted to surprise you with breakfast." She looks embarrassed as I try to salvage the nearly burnt bacon.

"It's perfect," I tell her, kissing her on the back of her head. She calls me a liar when I push her to the side and begin cooking the eggs beside the stove before she burns them too.

Spreading butter on her toast, I take a glimpse of her bare finger. Maybe it's time to give her something. "I love waking up and having breakfast with you," I tell her, trying to gauge how she's feeling about us.

"We should enjoy it before we have a house full of kids running around," she says, then giggles. She seems so happy lately, and she's thinking of our future. That's my sign this is the right time.

Excusing myself before heading into my bedroom, I open my night-stand drawer, taking a look at the item I bought before the incident with her father and his death.

A churning feeling in my stomach makes me hesitant when I rejoin her at the table. Her smile lights up the room, assuring me it's the right moment.

"Cora, are you happy with me?" I ask her, stalling.

"Always." Her eyes meet mine, and I know she means it.

Taking the box out of my pocket, I place it on the table in front of her. A shimmer of light passes through her eyes in anticipation. I open the box, displaying the purest and most beautiful diamond I could find, one that reminds me of her.

"Andrei!" she gasps. There's no reason for me to ask her for her hand. I already have it.

"I think it's time we make it official." I place the ring on her left finger. Several minutes go by as she admires it.

"It's beautiful, Andrei." She holds it up. It is definitely the best dia-mond money can buy. Still, it is not nearly as beautiful as the woman wearing it. It seems so unworthy of her.

"Not as beautiful as my fiancée," I reply. That sounds weird. She's been mine for a long time, but if I want to show her the respect a future Brigadier's wife deserves, I'll give her that name instead of sounding like I own her already.

I take a picture of the ring on her finger and send it to my mom. It was her idea.

"I have to tell you something," she says gingerly, pushing back her plate and fidgeting with the fork. She spends the next few minutes telling me about the book she wrote, what it contains and what she plans to do with it. My stomach lurches at what it is she's describing.

Not only did she write about our lives, but both her professor and editor have read it too. Why didn't she talk to me before taking those steps? A knot tightens in my stomach.

Cora has crossed a line by sharing our story with others. She should know better. We don't discuss our lives, let alone write about them for the world to read.

"Sorry, your book can never be published." Rage flows through me like lava. Standing, I throw the dirty dishes in the sink, and with my temper flaring, I pace around the kitchen.

"Andrei," she begins to respond, but I stop her.

"This is not up for discussion. You are my future wife. Now obey me like one." I attempt to grip her, but she pushes me away to run out of the condo. Immediately, I regret my words and begin to run after her but smack into someone standing outside, waiting for me.

"What are you doing here?" I ask him. *Why is my brother here?*

"Is this a bad time?" Dmitri asks as the sound of Cora slamming her door echoes through the hallway.

"You wouldn't understand." I stomp back into my kitchen and pour each of us a glass of vodka. Handing him a drink, I ask him again, "I said, what are you doing here?"

"I did some digging and found that Sasha has spent nearly $3 million of his money on a shell company," Dmitri informs me.

Feeling suffocated by this morning, I try to calm myself by taking deep breaths. Sasha is my only true friend, even more so than my brother standing before me. Growing up together, we always had each other's backs. I've trusted him with my life.

Sitting on the leather couch, I tilt my head back, holding the vodka bottle to my mouth. At this point, I'll be downing the entire thing within minutes. My eyes shoot over to Dmitri when he gives me a grunt. "What?"

"What if there's a way for Cora to publish her book, but we control what gets published?" His eyes narrow. Dmitri is the smartest Savin, always coming up with the brightest ideas.

"This is our life she's writing about. You know the rules." The first rule about being involved in organized crime is that you make sure the outside world doesn't know about your dealings.

"Give me a few days. She'll be back in love with you again," he promises. Dmitri places his glass on the table and then grabs the bottle from my hand. "Now get up. We have some work to do. Let's go find Sasha."

That's the thing with us brothers. We don't have to mask who we are. I'm safe being Andrei, the man who feels betrayed right now by both Belov twins and not a ruthless Brigadier. In my moments of weakness, my brothers aid me, guiding me into doing what must be done.

Opening Sasha's door, I find his messy room a reminder of what we had. With Dmitri in town, it's unlikely Sasha will see the sunrise tomorrow.

Chapter Thirty-Seven

SASHA

What a bloody mess on the floor, I think. The weight of my body, suspended by a rope tied around my wrist, causes the progressive tearing of my shoulders. The pain shoots up my arm like fire, then expands into the back of my head with a blinding whiteness that makes me lightheaded.

The stiffness in my neck makes looking up unbearable, but I can tell by the men's hushing that the boss is here. When Andrei first comes into view, I don't recognize the exterior mirrors of a ruthless man in front of me. I can't help but rewind to the happy memories I have with the man I consider my brother.

***

My knee began to bleed when I hit the ground, being no match for five boys. But I wasn't going to be a punk and not fight back. When one of the boys kicked me, I grabbed his leg, knocking him to the ground. The other four boys began punching me. I was starting to give up this fight when I heard a voice cry out, "Stop!"

The boys backed away, and I looked up to find a pair of hazel eyes staring down at me.

"You're lucky we're scared of your dad," one of the boys called out.

"You should be scared of me," the boy said. He stepped over me and then, with a closed fist, punched one of the boys in the face. The boy grabbed his bleeding nose and ran away, his friends not far behind him.

"Thanks," I told him. As he reached out his hand, I grabbed it and stood up, giving him a look.

This boy was different from those at my new school. He even dressed differently with his ironed khaki pants and polo shirt. This boy cared about how he looked.

"You're new here," he said in a statement. We began to walk down the hallway.

"What grade are you in?" We were both the same size, but he had an older demeanor about him.

"Kindergarten," he replied.

"I'm..." I began to tell him when he cut me off.

"You're Sasha Belov," he said.

"Who's your father?" If he recognized me, our fathers must work together.

"That's not important." We reached our classroom, and my new friend asked me, "Do you want to sit next to me?" I looked across the room when the five boys who'd beaten me up walked in. Nodding, I took the desk next to my new friend.

It was my first day at my new school in New York. I had just arrived from Russia with my father. My sister Cora wouldn't be coming until a few months later, leaving me to fend for myself. So, I could use a friend.

The teacher began class with attendance. When she called out, "Savin," my jaw dropped when I realized who I had just made friends with.

"You're Andrei Savin!" I gasped.

He turned to me with a smirk and winked.

***

Andrei's face is but an inch from mine. His hazel eyes are cold and sharp as winter water. When he takes a step back, Dmitri's fist punches me in the gut. He continues striking me with repeated blows until my side seizes up.

"Why are you doing this to me?" I shout in between spasms, looking from one to the other. Their silence sends chills down my spine.

A sharp blade pokes my skin as the man behind me cuts the ropes, releasing me. My body lies in a slimy pool of my own blood on the freezing concrete. Dmitri slams his foot down on my face.

In one shattered moment, my heart and breathing stopped. The black consumes me until I can't feel the pain anymore.

I don't wake until dawn comes. I can barely move, my body struggling to recover, to repair the damage. I can't recall how long the beating went on, only bringing to mind the final kick and the sound of Andrei's voice ordering Dmitri to stop.

I trace the scar around my wrist with my finger. At least I'm no longer bound. As I scan the room, I spot Andrei leaning against the wall, watching me. Even though he's the one responsible for my suffering, a part of me feels relieved he didn't abandon me.

With a clenched jaw, Andrei speaks. "You've betrayed me, brother."

I'm baffled by his statement. What can he mean? I have been loyal to him my entire life. Killing my family and anyone associated with my surname should guarantee my loyalty to Andrei. I would do anything for him. "What are you talking about?"

"We know you're the one working against my family," he says in a low voice as though knowing this for certain. But it's not true and I don't see how he can even think that!

I know about the uprising in the Coalition against the Savin family. What did they think would happen if they were to kill one of its associates? The Savins had to have known not everyone would be happy with the power they had been flexing this past summer. But when the rumbling got too close to my ear, I made it known that I would not go against Andrei, and they stopped gossiping to me. So, I am not the perpetrator, not the one who has been working against them.

"I consider you a brother. Why do you think I would side with men who want to harm you and your family?" I ask him curiously and with sincerity.

"I know about the money you've been spending and your meetings with the professor," he mutters with a crumpling face.

I begin to feel some assurance I may make it to see nightfall. "That's what this is about?" I sigh before lying across the floor, laughing.

"I'm glad you find this funny," Andrei says, annoyed.

"That you're an idiot? Yes!" Looking up, I'm reminded of the pain Andrei put me through last night as the rope dangles from the ceiling. "And you're a fucking asshole for what you did to me last night!"

"Stop with the secrets," he says, speaking through his teeth.

"I can't tell you—." Before I finish, Andrei grabs me, lifting me to my feet. With a furrowed brow, he glares at me, mouth opened as if lost for words. "But I can show you," I tell him.

"You think I would trust you?" he asks me.

"If you want to know my secrets, we'll have to go on a little field trip," I say with caution.

"If you screw with me, Sasha, I won't think twice about putting a round of bullets in your head." Andrei releases me.

When we get into the car, my reflection in the mirror is daunting. Andrei has never questioned my loyalty, and I'm beginning to feel an emotional roller coaster. There is damage to my skin, yet the bruising to my heart will take far longer than that to heal.

"We need to stop and get Cora. You both need to see this," I tell him with disappointment.

Chapter Thirty-Eight

ANDREI

We are far from Seattle, the road stretching onward, winding around the mountain stream until we finally reach a muddy driveway. The pathway here is desolate, with plenty of bends and curves. The ground is still very muddy from the recent rain. At the end of the road sits a cottage.

Michael stands beside the parked car, gripping his gun until he clearly sees us pulling in. I wave him off and open the door to let Cora out of the vehicle. She avoids making eye contact with me, concentrating solely on Sasha as he steps slowly out of our vehicle.

He tries to say Cora's name, but his cracked lips fail at the first letter. Cora is already running to him, her eyes jolting from one injury to another.

He walks like a scarecrow more than a man. His left eye is swollen, and he can't see a thing out of it and probably won't for a while. His clothes are an utter mess with dried bloodstains. He'll have to cut his clothes away from his body.

"What the hell, Andrei?" she screams at me.

"Calm down," Sasha interjects.

She tries to hold him in her arms, but he pushes her away, grunting in pain. Her squeeze is too much for his multiple cracked ribs.

"Someone tell me what's going on," she commands both of us.

As always, Sasha manages Cora for me. "It was business." He offers her comfort by slipping his arm around her shoulder.

She snuggles into him before whispering in his ear, "Did he do this to you?"

"No," Sasha answers her.

I feel incredibly ashamed of my distrust of my friend. The thought I could do this to my brother breaks something inside me. There is sadness in his eyes, a heaviness and unyielding sorrow that shows in his smile.

I attempt to break the tension by asking, "What are we doing here, Sasha?"

He gestures and starts walking toward the house. As I walk by Cora, she grabs my hand and tells me, gritting her teeth, "If I find out you did that to him, we're over."

We follow him down a track, beaten by feet, not specially constructed. It's surrounded by trees and flowers, and one can feel the freshness of the breeze. The house, tucked away in the woods, is easy to overlook. Before us stands a cozy, wood-sided home probably one of the smallest I've ever seen.

When I enter the unfamiliar place, I step into a comfortable, home-like living room. I immediately notice a picture of the Belov twins and myself over the wood fireplace.

"What the fuck is this?" I ask, narrowing my eyes to a door that's caught Cora's attention.

A shrill cry can be heard in the room. I run to Cora, finding her browsing the built-in bookshelves.

"Is this for me?" She turns and asks Sasha, admiring the little library, stroking a finger down the spines of many of the old books carefully placed there.

"It's for both of you," he answers her, standing in the doorway. "I was saving it for your wedding, but I guess I can give it to you now."

"You bought my dream house," she gushes. I faintly remember our conversation about Cora's desire to have a little cabin in the woods where she would have the solitude to write her stories. I couldn't understand why she would want something so small when we grew up in the most lavish places in New York and Russia. But Cora has always enjoyed the quietness the library offers, so I'm not surprised this would be what Cora chooses for herself.

"Great, you bought us 'this' house," I say sounding displeased, and rolling my eyes.

"No. I bought Cora this house. I got you something even more special," Sasha says, his voice trailing away as he disappears through the back door. We follow him.

Situated at the back of the cottage is a little shed followed by a layer of forest trees. The inside is filled with everything you might need to upkeep the garden—rakes, shovels, a lawnmower, and hedge trimmers. I chuckle at the thought that Sasha would think I'd take up yard work.

Sensing my lack of excitement, Sasha moves a piece of equipment, revealing a hidden button. When he clicks it, the ground below us moves. Buried under a pile of fertilizer is a secret door.

Standing near the edge, I squint down the hole, unable to see the end. "You first," I command Sasha. As he begins to descend the ladder, Dmitri jumps in front of me, following him.

"Stay here," I tell Cora.

"Not a chance," she tells me, one foot already stepping onto the ladder.

Now, I have no choice but to descend into the secret passage. "Sasha, why can't we see anything?" I call out into the darkness.

"It's part of the security feature," I hear his voice echo.

"If we die, I'm going to come back alive and kill you all over," I threaten him before feeling my shoe touch the ground. The area is bleak, cold, and completely dark.

"Boo!" I hear Sasha whisper, making Cora scream. Before I can pull my gun out of my pants, a light illuminates, revealing a metal door.

Sasha presses the buttons on a metal panel next to the door.

We enter another dark square room, with only a single light cast upon another security box. "The code is our birthday," he tells Cora, pressing the buttons.

To my surprise, the door opens, and the room comes into full view, one lightbulb at a time. "Oh, shit!" Dmitri shouts.

After admiring the bunker for several minutes, I ask Sasha, "What is this?"

"Your new safe house," he answers, standing beside me with a smug smile. He did good, very good. I walk around the bunker to find everything we would need to hide for months, maybe a year. The bunker has a kitchen, sitting room, bedroom, and a storage room full of canned and dry foods and water. Hidden behind a wall is a whole armory of weapons.

Sasha explains that he needed the professor's expertise to run the bunker on solar panels, hydropower, and batteries. The well-built concrete shelter twenty feet underground would survive a nuke attack.

"I know where I'm going in case of a zombie apocalypse," Cora chuckles and we all join her.

"We are going to make so much money," Dmitri chimes in. "Imagine what the Pakhan and other Brigadiers would pay for a bunker like this." He's not wrong.

Sasha may not have intended this to be a new business venture for us, but he has unwittingly created a new income stream and an improved cash flow for the Savins.

"Good job." I take his hand in a handshake, then go in for an embrace. He flinches when I hug him. I can't say I blame him.

"Sasha, I'm ..."

He cuts me off. "Brigadiers, don't apologize," he whispers to me softly, so Cora doesn't hear.

Sasha has always been reliable and supportive, demonstrating unwavering loyalty to my family. Healing the hurt I've caused him will take time, but I hope my words convey just how remorseful I am for my actions.

"But brothers do. I'm sorry."

Chapter Thirty-Nine

ANDREI

"You ready for me?" I whisper in her ear, licking her cum off my lips. She gives me a slight nod and a soft sound escapes her. Hearing her moan makes my cock even harder.

Cora leans against the window, arms spread open, my naked Kitten standing vulnerable and available for the city to see. The lights from the city brighten up the room, but we're still somewhat concealed with just the corner light on.

With her hair tangled in my fingers, I give it a slight pull, pushing her head further into the window. The tensing of her shoulders is an indication she knows I'm about to be rough.

My hardened cock rubs between the crack of her firm ass, the feeling of her skin rubbing against me only tormenting me more. I ate her pussy so good that Cora screamed over and over again and came twice on my face. Watching her and feeling her wetness around my mouth causes a strain so severe I just want to come and come hard.

I jerk off my cock with a few pumps until the precum drips onto my fingers. Wrapping my hand around her waist, I pull Cora up onto her toes and, without warning, ram my cock into her tight pussy. My Kitten isn't ready and lets out a loud shriek.

I don't let up, moving my hands to hold her tits as she arches her back further. She meets me thrust for thrust, my cock slamming into her hard enough to make her scream with each thrust. My fuck is hard and fast, looking for instant gratification.

It's been days since I slipped the ring onto my new fiancée's finger, only for her to betray me. The pain of Cora prioritizing herself over my family and our future together still lingers. I'm still angry with her, thinking of her selfishness. I'm taking out that anger on her at this very moment as our bodies bang against each other.

A light from the hotel across the street catches my attention, and I see someone watching us. Cora's head is turned, looking at me. I tighten my fingers around her hair to prevent her from looking back out the window and seeing the man watching. Instead, I pull her closer to me and only fuck her harder, staring directly at the man. If he wants a show, then I'll give him one.

"Play with yourself," I order her. A finger slips across my balls as Cora begins to tickle her pussy. I can tell how hard she's playing with her clit by the way her hips move in sync with her fingers.

She's so fucking wet, her pussy juices drip on my cock. "Come for me, Kitten," I tell her, eager to feel her getting more soaked from her own orgasm.

"Fuck me," she bites out before her scream rings in the air. The sound of my Kitten's pleasure with the feeling of her pussy tightening and squeezing around me makes my cock stiffen.

After a few more thrusts into her, it becomes difficult to hold back. With my excitement increasing to the point of no return, my semen begins to spurt into her, followed by another and another. Once I start coming, I have no control over it until I tilt my head backward, sighing and trying to catch my breath.

The man still watches, and I give him a polite wave, without Cora noticing. She would be too embarrassed. But I don't care. *I'm the fucking king!*

"Andrei!" Cora pants with a soft chuckle. When I pull out of her, I find myself with a big mess of cum on me. Still holding her tight, I guide us both to the shower to clean each other up.

Cora takes a few extra minutes in there, and I glance back at her, watching her wipe the soap off her small breasts. My cock hardens, signaling it might be time for another round.

I had planned this night away for the two of us to reconnect. My mother was right in picking Cora as a Brigadier's wife. Because she's grown up in this life, when I told her the book deal was dead, she didn't argue, only disagreed. It's not that I don't want to support my future wife in her passion. But, as a future Bratva leader, I must make hard decisions that are best for the Bratva and our family, not just each individual. However, I can still feel her holding some resentment towards me.

A glass of vodka dangles from my hand as I walk to the window. The stars descend from the night sky, creating a pathway of lustrous lights bouncing off the tall buildings. Even in its current beauty, it's no comparison to home.

"This could all be yours if you wanted it." Cora wraps her arms around my chest, her perky nipples on my back.

She's right. There are no significant players here in the Pacific Northwest. It's one of the reasons why my family has been coming here for years.

My history with Seattle started as a little boy. My brothers and I asked our father if we could learn to hunt. With five boys running around the house, our mother convinced my dad that outdoor activities would help us get some of our energy out. But, when you're Russian mafia royalty, you just can't take an ordinary hunting vacation, so my dad built a compound in Washington with fifty acres of hunting grounds.

We continued to buy different properties all throughout the Pacific Northwest until the cartel felt we were getting too close to their California territory and, in the middle of the night, burnt down our house while our mother was sleeping, barely escaping with her life. That's when my father sold off all his West Coast properties. I imagine the memory of almost losing his wife is one of the reasons why my father hates me being in Seattle.

Those vacations were my favorite childhood memories with my dad and brothers. And that's how I want Seattle to remain—good memories. Also, with our new cottage, I can bet Cora will want to spend time here, and someday, that will include new memories with our children.

If I bring Bratva business to Seattle, the gray clouds will release crimson rain to the streets. But blood had already been shed when Cora's father tried to kill me.

With my new partnership with the professor, it's only a matter of time before other organized crime families infiltrate Seattle to get a piece for themselves. Cora's right; it's time that Seattle's veil gets pierced, and if I want to preserve those happy memories, I should own the city before the cartel encroaches up north. It's time Seattle fell under Bratva territory.

More specifically, mine.

Chapter Forty

ANDREI

I lived in *El Grande* my entire life, but still, the basement feels like unknown territory. I killed my first man here on my thirteenth birthday, a rat who turned on my family and the Coalition, so it was an easy decision for me to make. Still, I remember my hands shaking and the thoughts that ran through my mind after he took his last breath.

It doesn't matter how many men you've watched die; taking a man's life for the first time is something you don't forget. Other teenage boys would have felt guilt or regret, but not a future Brigadier. The gun I held tightly in my hands gave me power. Not the power I was born with, but the power of becoming a Bratva man, who I was meant to be.

It's a hectic day in the basement as the Coalition gathers in the Boardroom, the Bratva's equivalent of a town hall meeting. The Pakhan, Brigadiers, and the Colonel all sit up front while the Bratva leaders fill the room to discuss or vote on various topics.

There are strict rules in the Boardroom. One of them is that you can only attend if you are invited. I started attending these meetings last year when the Pakhan personally invited me. Because my father is the current Brigadier, I'm nearly a bystander, unable to vote or have a say.

Another important rule is that no weapons except the Coalition's Army are allowed. Colonel Lev is the leader of our Army. He and his men protect the Pakhan and Brigadiers. The Colonel reports directly to the Pakhan, and his orders come straight from the top.

He is one sick motherfucker and kills for sport. His main weaknesses are his lack of intent and strategy, and the fact that he has no sons. When he retires, by choice or death, we will need a new Colonel. Lucky for me, Colonel Lev has taken a particular interest in my brother Nikolai, and I intend for him to sit in his seat one day. Two Savins at the head of the table will make us nearly untouchable in the Bratva.

I sit near the front of the room, as close as I'm allowed near my father. Nikolai is able to join at the request of the Colonel but doesn't join me. Instead, he stands with his back to the wall, watching the men in the room.

The closest person to me is my best friend, Sasha. When his father died, the Belov seat was passed on to him. It's his first time in the Boardroom, and I place my hand on his shaking knee to calm him down. The men are whispering about us. I ignore them, but they've got Sasha on edge.

We have many enemies because of what we did to the Belov family. The only reason the leaders of the Coalition haven't given an order to punish us is because Sasha's dad intended to hurt me. Their backing is out of respect for my dad, but that still doesn't keep the lower-ranking men from wanting revenge. They think the Savins are gaining too much power—a power we take away from them.

The Pakhan enters the room, and the chatter immediately stops as the entire room of organized crime leaders stands. Even in the world's largest Bratva, the men know when to follow the rules. The most important rule is that you always show respect to the Pakhan.

Assorted topics get discussed, and my mind wanders away bored as I begin to think of Cora. We left her in Seattle with Dmitri nearby if anything happened while I was out. I'm hoping this meeting doesn't last long so I can hurry to the airport and have Cora wake in my arms. I've practically tuned out all the talking until Sasha hits my arm, causing me to jolt. That's when I realized the discussion had become about me.

"We're going to award Seattle to a boy who killed one of our own?" a man in the back asks. I recognize him as someone I've seen before but don't know him.

My father begins to answer the question, but Sasha jumps in before he does. My best friend will always defend me, even at the wrong time. "Andrei has made Seattle profitable to the Coalition. He has a right to claim the city."

"You're just a boy. Your view doesn't matter." The man laughs at Sasha, and others join him.

My godfather jumps in to stop the laughter from spreading across the room by asking the crowd, "What have you done on the West Coast to make us rich?"

The men who were laughing only seconds ago sit silently. None of them have made the Coalition as much money as I plan to in the upcoming years. The leaders of the Bratva know my worth, and it's not based on what I've done so far but on what I can do for them in the future.

Then, in a room so quiet you could hear a pin drop, a man yells, "Punish the boy!" A bunch of men join him, and I can't see who yelled first. The crowd begins to stand, screaming at the Pakhan about him not being fair and unbiased since he's my uncle. I look at him and my father, and they have both become agitated with the crowd.

"Stop!" my father roars, trying to be heard across the room, but it makes the men even madder, and they begin yelling profanities even louder. A chair flies across the room, aiming at my father so fast that I can't tell where it came from.

Colonel Lev and the Army jump into security mode and guard the Pakhan and the Brigadiers while escorting them out of the room through the back door. Before my father leaves, he hesitates, looking back at me.

I nod for him to get out, his safety far more important than mine. A man begins to rush me, his face red and hand scrunched up in a ball. I stand ready to fight him but don't have to. From the side, Nikolai comes hurrying, rushing the man and tackling him to the ground. Other men try to help the man by pushing Nikolai off of him as his fist continues to hit the man's face, splattering blood all over the floor, soon to transform into a spreading red pool.

I grab my brother by the shoulder, lift him to his feet, and shove him through the crowd. We need to make a quick exit before one of us gets hurt. Sasha joins us as we exit. We quickly head down the hall toward the elevator, the door closing before the men catch up with us.

The ride to the 56th floor lasts forever. I tap the back of my head against the metal wall. *What happened in there?*

Sasha sighs. "The men are just scared."

"Those motherfuckers are dead," Nikolai growls, wiping the blood from his hand on his shirt.

"No, Sasha's right," I jump in. A lot has happened this summer. They just need time.

"They could have hurt you," Nikolai bites out.

"But they didn't," I remind him. The last thing we need is for Nikolai to start kicking down doors and shooting people.

Sasha lets out a deep sigh. "They're just scared of change. Andrei will change the Bratva one day and they know when he does, he'll be the most powerful Brigadier the Coalition has ever had."

I've wanted to do things in the Bratva differently to increase our profits, adding business ventures organized criminals haven't begun exploring. As long as I was making the men money, I thought they'd support the change, never considering it would be what they feared.

"Look, whatever we do, we do together." Sasha holds his fist in the air. "Together," we all say simultaneously bumping our fists against each other's.

As the elevator doors slide open, relief washes over us, and our security team stands at the ready, weapons drawn. But as they see us step out, they quickly holster their guns. Sasha and I enter the Savin apartment first, my hands still trembling from the incident.

Sasha places his hand on my forearm, whispering, "Together." A new era in the Bratva is coming, and we will do it together.

Chapter Forty-One

CORA

The words on paper are just that—words, one keystroke after another, none of them put together to make any coherent thought or idea. My frustration over my book has killed my motivation to write. *Why bother putting a story on paper if no one will read it?*

The editor for the publishing company keeps reaching out, and the phone rings and rings unanswered. I keep declining her calls to avoid telling her I won't be moving forward with my book. At this point, her messages are becoming annoying, so when the phone rings again, I take a deep breath and answer, prepared to tell her my bad news.

"Oh! You finally answered," the voice on the line screams out.

Before I can apologize for wasting her time while not sharing the reason for my rude avoidance, she cuts back in. "The new president of our publishing company is in the office today and is demanding to see you immediately."

"New president?" The company is less than a year old. That's why I was willing to work with them. Big companies ask too many questions. After a few minutes of begging and inferring she might be fired if I don't come in, I reluctantly agree.

Michael drops me off on the corner of Main Street before looking for a parking space. It's hard to find a spot at this hour as people dine in the small town's restaurants during lunchtime. Weaving between the local business-people, I stop short of a little office in the middle of town. The outside got an updated paint job with a new awning covering the windows. It's got a modern twist compared to the older offices next door and along the street.

When I enter, the young lady glances up from her computer, surprised to see me. "You came!"

"You asked me to," I retort, rolling my eyes in annoyance. It would have been much easier if I'd just blocked her number.

"Like I said, we were recently bought by a guy interested in book publishing," she says, speaking loudly over her clicking heels as she escorts me to the back office.

The office has been remodeled since I visited last week. The new modern furniture reminds me of New York, where minimalism is the latest trend. White open workstations fill the outer space of the office, and an ample lounge filled with white leather couches was added in the middle. The wall, painted black with all-white art pieces, is reminiscent of a city art gallery.

Excitedly, the lady barely knocks before entering the office at the end of the hall, immediately regretting it. In front of us is the new president, fucking one of the young interns across his desk. Neither of them notices us as the man begins to groan, pulling his cock out of her before coming all over her ass.

The young new editor of mine yelps, "I'm so sorry." The man behind the desk isn't bothered by the intrusion, grabbing a tissue to wipe his hands.

The blonde intern bending over the desk doesn't even bother to wipe his cum off of her before pulling down her dress. The two ladies quickly exit, embarrassed to look at me or the new boss.

"I see you've made yourself at home quickly," I tell the new president as he sits across the desk smugly, not the least surprised by what I just saw. This isn't my first time walking in on him with a young lady. The young man in front of me is quite charming and enjoys the ladies a little too much.

"I thought you would be more excited to see me, Cora," Dmitri Savin says with a grin.

I muster a faint smile in return. The Savin men might be my future brothers-in-law, but make no mistake, they are killers. The one sitting across from me just happens to be the smartest one.

"Cora, what were you thinking writing a book like this?" he asks with piercing eyes. So, I've upset more than Andrei with my book.

"What are you doing here, Dmitri?"

Dmitri goes into a long-winded explanation about asking his father to buy him this boutique publishing company for his recent eighteenth birthday.

Why would Dmitri want to own this company? It won't generate the billions of dollars the Savin businesses own.

"I like books," he replies, but he's lying. Dmitri reads the latest business and financial books to keep his mind sharp, but this is a romance book publishing company. He wouldn't know a good romance story if it hit him over the head.

Sitting back in the chair, I fold my arms and roll my eyes.

Waving his hands in the air, he finally confesses, "Fine! Sasha gave you both a great wedding gift, and I wanted to give you something special. This way, you get your book published and a job as an editor if you want it."

"And Andrei?" I ask him.

"He gets a happy wife!" He slides a book across the desk, and I lean in for a better look. The cover is alluring, featuring the title of my book embossed on it. The author's name is one I don't recognize. "Julie Larkins?"

"You didn't think you could publish a book under the name Cora Savin, did you?" Sounding annoyed, he huffs. "If you want to be an author, Cora, this is the only way."

With Dmitri as the company's owner, he will have complete control of my work. But he'll also have control over maintaining my anonymity.

"Cora, we have to protect Andrei. He's the priority, even above us," Dmitri tells me authoritatively. "As his future wife, you will understand that."

Everything the Savin family does is about Andrei. Dmitri and Nikolai's entire existence has been about protecting their future Brigadier. They place him before themselves. They always have and always will.

Holding a Brigadier spot is exclusive in the Coalition. Only the founding families hold those, so the Savins have a lot of enemies. If the Savin family falls, the domino effect can happen, destroying the largest Bratva in the world.

Protecting Andrei is not about protecting Andrei, the man. It's about protecting the family, the family name, and the family's immense fortune.

I push the book back toward Dmitri. It was very kind of him to do this for me, but I won't be accepting his offer.

"I appreciate this, Dmitri. I really do. But I need to do this on my own," my shaking voice makes me sound like a little girl disappointing her family.

"Hmm, I see," he says curiously with his chin in his fingers, his eyes staring into mine as to read my thoughts. I can never think about outsmarting him. He's very clever, even more so than Andrei. "You plan to leave him."

I press my lips together, holding back a response. I'm still weighing my options, but deep down, I yearn to carve out my own path and have something that belongs solely to me. *This book was mine! How dare they mess with the one thing I still own!*

"He'll never let you go, Cora. You belong to the Coalition, you belong to our family, you belong to him," Dmitri calmly tells me, but I'm not listening. First, I belonged to my father. Now, I belong to Andrei. At what stage does any of these men realize I need to belong to myself?

The thought of never living the life I want overwhelms me, and I don't want to hear any more of this garbage. My legs move fast as I run out of the building, past the people on the sidewalk, until I run smack into Michael around the corner.

You belong to him still echoes in my ear.

Chapter Forty-Two

ANDREI

Right before I reach her clit, I apply more pressure against her, slowing my movement. Her breaths are shallow, and she is on the edge of coming, but I'm not ready to taste her cum yet.

I've been eating her pussy so long my tongue has become somewhat numb, each time bringing her close to climaxing, then slowing and backing off so she doesn't. Yeah, I know I'm an asshole, but I love her vanilla sugar cookies tasting pussy, and I'm the fucking monster who can't eat enough of it.

Two of my fingers dip into her pussy slowly. Cora thrusts her hip upwards, begging for more. *Who am I to deny my fiancée what she wants?* Obliging her request, I use my longest finger to give her a deeper penetration until the tip of my nail touches a part of her vagina wall. She lets out a squeal. Seems I've hit the spot. I keep my fingers right where they are and turn my attention back to licking her.

My tongue presses against her harder, flicking her clit with just the tip. Cora lets out a deep moan, and then her fingers tangle in my hair. With force, she pushes my face into her, and I'm no longer in control. She's drowning me in her wet pussy, and I'm loving it, my Kitten on the brink of exploding.

My cock is so fucking hard, it hurts. I'm battling my need for release and wanting to see her begging for more. "Please!" Cora begs, her voice strained. With a growl, my teeth nibble on her clit, and my fingers dig into her pussy further. It only takes a few seconds before she arches her back, and her moans fill the air.

I can't bear the strain any longer, not waiting for her to finish before replacing my fingers with my cock. Her warmth hugs it, and her natural lube feels like wet silk. With every thrust, her pussy pulsates tightly around me. Cora's pussy fits perfectly around my cock like two pieces of a puzzle snapping together. She has the perfect pussy for a future king!

It doesn't take long before my cum spills into her. I don't pull out until every last drop is inside of Cora. I lay my weak body on top of her, hugging her and enjoying the smell of her expensive perfume with my nose nestled into her neck. She drapes her arms over me, closing her eyes.

Sitting up on my elbow, I pause to look at her face. Cora is so beautiful, not that made-up prettiness the young girls are doing today with all those revolting fake surgeries, but naturally beautiful. She's grown up a lot since we were five, but all the same features are there. I think of her at that age with hazel eyes. Our daughter will have her beauty with my eyes. I will have to kill every man who ever thinks of looking at her.

"What are you thinking about?" she asks, catching me staring.

"Our future kids," I reply, loving how her face lights up like a Christmas tree.

As much as I love coming in her, I'm not ready for kids anytime soon. Cora and I are on the same page about this. I get a brief every time Cora sees the doctor, and I know she's been taking birth control pills. I reassured myself of this fact by looking through her bathroom and finding a half-empty pill pack.

Sliding from the bed, I amble into the kitchen for a water bottle. It's only been a few weeks since Sasha gifted us this cottage, and Cora has already completely decorated the place as though planning to live here permanently.

"You've done a good job with the place," I tell her as she joins me in the kitchen.

"Just giving it a feminine touch," she says with a dashing smile. Grabbing her book, she tucks herself under a blanket. I join her on the couch, scratching my head and thinking.

"Andrei, what's going on?" Laying her book down, she grabs my hand.

"Something is always going on in our world," I reply with a polite smile. I lock my fingers into hers.

She rolls her eyes, annoyed.

I tilt my head away from her. That's the problem when you're with someone you've known your entire life; they can feel when something is wrong. No words or expressions are needed. They just know.

"First, our night in the hotel room and now our new cottage." She pulls my face to her.

It's time I have this conversation with her. "Cora, I've enjoyed my time here in Seattle with you. However, my place is in New York, next to my father." It's been nice to have this time away from our families and everyone, just the two of us here together, but it was never permanent. I've been in Seattle too long and on borrowed time.

"You're leaving me?" she asks, dropping her fingers from my face and looking away.

Her question hits me harder than I expected. How could she even consider that I might leave her? She knows we're meant to be together. I've given her a ring, after all. "Never. You're my future wife. You're going with me."

She pulls away from me, walking into the kitchen. "What if I say no?"

I follow her. She doesn't look at me as she begins washing dishes and wiping the counter, as if trying to inject tension into the air between us.

Have I not made myself clear to her this past year? Have I not made it clear that we both have responsibilities we need to fill? I am responsible for my family, our businesses, and the Coalition. Cora was raised to be a Coalition wife. I didn't make the rules or promise her to me, but I will fulfill my obligation to the agreement. That's what is expected of a future Brigadier.

I know my following statement will hurt her, but it's time Cora grew up a little and stopped this nonsense of a fantasy she's living here in Seattle. It's time for Cora to realize our lives have already been decided, and they are intertwined, enmeshed to a degree that will make it impossible to separate us.

"My fiancée will be by my side when I return home. You decide if you're going willingly or by force," I bite into my words forcefully, informing her I'm not playing this game anymore. I don't wait for an answer, slamming the front door on departing the cottage.

Chapter Forty-Three

SASHA

Her long legs tightening around my neck choke me with every orgasm. My blond cheerleader has the tightest pussy that continues to pulsate around my cock, squeezing around me. I take a deep breath, trying not to come yet, but every time her friend's tongue touches my cock, I find it hard to control myself. There seems to be no end to my cum, continually spurting each time one of them titillates me just that little bit more.

Amy's screams echo through the room, followed by her friend's moans. There is nothing sexier than watching two cheerleaders licking and nibbling each other while my cock is deep inside one of them, filling her up, throbbing before I dare to explode—then doing it again and again.

Amy has been the best thing about college. I followed Andrei to Seattle, providing him protection, but I was never interested in getting a degree or doing anything with one.

I arrived in Seattle last year unwillingly and ready to go home. As for Andrei, he was too busy winning Cora over to have fun with me, so he ordered me to find my own party. So, that's what I did. The best thing to emerge from the one frat party I attended was meeting my sexy cheerleader, the one I have continued to see at every possible opportunity.

Amy is fun and adventurous, and I mean in the bedroom, often inviting her sorority sisters to join us in bed.

My cock has swelled, and I can't hold it in any longer. "I'm about to come!" I push the girl off Amy, fisting my cock. Both girls kneel below me on the bed as I jerk off and come on both of their faces. The girls swap my cum with a kiss until I've spilled every last drop.

My body feels as though I got hit by a dump truck. Lying in her bed, I watch Amy and her friend clean up. The two girls walk around naked, wiping my cum from their bodies. I don't try to hide my dick that's somehow rising yet again as I watch two sexy girls' tits bouncing.

Once we're alone, Amy moves over to the bed, hovering over me. "So, when do you return from New York?" she asks. I had let her know I would be gone for a while. Of course, we argued over it because she wanted to come with me. There was absolutely no chance I was showing up at Andrei's birthday party with her as my date.

I'm excited to finally return home. Our place is in New York. With the looming threat over Andrei, I don't need to worry about Amy being around the Coalition. Leaving her here in Seattle is the best thing for her.

"I don't know," I answer her honestly because the reality is I go where Andrei tells me to.

"I'll miss you," she complains as she places her lips on mine. Our tongues interlock, swapping spit.

"I'll miss you, too." I reciprocate her sentiment. It's not totally a lie. Amy is the only girl I've gotten close to in a while. When things slow down, I'll fly her to the city for a visit.

I can't stand my hurting dick any longer, pushing Amy over and heading to the bathroom to piss. Holding myself up with one arm against the wall, I take my time to shake myself off.

"Move!" Amy pushes me from the toilet, making me piss a residual trickle on myself.

"What the fuck?" I yell at her as I shake the piss off my hands.

Before I have even flushed, Amy kneels over the toilet, throwing up. After washing my hands off, I stand there holding her hair while she pukes for a few more minutes.

"Are you sick?" She seemed fine when I left her in bed.

"I'm fine," she chokes out, finally finishing.

I leave her alone in the bathroom to clean herself, and she nestles back into her bed. "How long have you been throwing up?" I ask her, hoping this is the first time.

"A few weeks," she says nervously. *A few weeks?*

"You're not pregnant, are you?" Inside, my heart races in my ribcage as if it's trying to escape.

When we started fucking, she told me I didn't have to use protection because she was on the pill, and I was the only guy she was sleeping with. I took that as an invitation to fuck her raw and fuck her often. I've never asked again since. But I should have known better and used condoms. *Fuck! How could I have been so stupid?*

"I missed a few pills," she cries out to me. She knows she's fucked up.

"Accidentally or on purpose?" I ask her, my big hand gripping both sides of her face.

"Let me go!" She smacks my hands off of her.

"While I'm gone, you better go to the doctor," I order her. "And call me right after."

Amy agrees. I'll follow up later for a date and time.

One thing I really appreciate about Amy is her knack for turning an angry man's mood around. She's always been my go-to stress reliever. It's strange, though—right now, even though she's the source of my stress, she still has the power to calm me down. That's why I've spent so much time with her over the last year. All the bullshit going on in the Coalition has had me on edge way more than any nineteen-year-old man should be.

But she doesn't know what I do for a living. She just knows I work for Andrei, a wealthy businessman. When she starts to ask questions, I buy her a nice piece of jewelry to shut her up. We both benefit from this relationship.

Sensing my agitation, she kisses me one peck at a time, starting at my mouth and moving down to my groin. I slap her face with my cock a few times before opening her mouth with my thumb. She nibbles on me playfully as if she might bite it off before I daringly do stick my dick between her teeth. Sucking me off instead, she asks in between mouthfuls, "Forgive me?"

I don't know if I can forgive her, but this is a good start. "Maybe after you swallow my cum," my voice growls. I grab her head and shove my cock further down her throat until she chokes.

Chapter Forty-Four

CORA

This luxurious mansion is very busy this afternoon. Usually, security around the property hides in the shadows, but today, they are in full force out in the open, checking every corner and edge of the perimeter.

It usually doesn't bother me much having men with guns watching my every move. Of course, it's all I've ever known, so I ignore them and go about my day as usual. But I've grown to enjoy Seattle, a place where security is limited.

I scurry across the formal living room, looking for my mom, who I've just heard has arrived. I almost bump into one of the housekeepers, anxiously scrubbing the floor. I tip-toed across the floor, trying not to dirty it, looking down at my reflection.

Mrs. Savin has gone all out for Andrei's twentieth birthday party. Usually, these parties aren't for the birthday boys but more for the Savins to keep up their appearances as the absolute best business leaders in New York.

The brothers grew up with high-ranking business and political sons, forming a vital part of the elite group of wealthy young men in New York.

When I talk about being wealthy, I'm not referring to the newly minted rich who just landed their first jobs on Wall Street. Having a few million dollars won't get you into this exclusive fraternity. The money of this group of young men goes back generations and amounts to billions of dollars.

Finally, I enter the kitchen to find my mother and Mrs. Savin standing around the breakfast bar, drinking coffee and making pastries for tonight. Although a giant birthday cake was ordered for the party, Mrs. Savin thought it would be great to make a few homemade treats for the boys since all the brothers would be home together for a few days.

I grab an apron from the chef's pantry and jump in to help. Growing up, I often joined my mom in baking different types of Russian pastries in the kitchen. I can't cook dinner or fry bacon but make an excellent Napolean cake.

This is the first time I've seen my mom since my father's death. I hug her, quickly noticing how frail she had become due to losing a good amount of weight on her already thin body.

She had told me many times over the phone that she did not blame or hate me for my father's death. My father knew his actions would have consequences. But my mother had not offered me or my brother any comfort either.

She hadn't said one negative thing about my father, even though he'd tried to kill his own kids. I don't know if it's because my mother had been raised in this lifestyle, but it's as if she's immune to the terrible things that happen to our family.

Nikolai enters the kitchen. It's impossible to miss him since he's by far the tallest and most heavily built of all the brothers at sixteen.

He just strides past his mom, giving her a polite hug before grabbing me and pulling me into the air. "Nikolai!" I scream with laughter. "Put me down."

Out of all the brothers, I have the closest relationship with him. While his older brothers played football outside, I would sit with him, watching TV and playing. I even taught him how to read. When either of us is crossed, we rely on each other and can talk freely to one another about it without judgment. In a way, we're kind of best friends.

The twin brothers run past us in the kitchen, yelling their hellos before running outside and jumping into the pool, water splashing everywhere. Mrs. Savin yells at them. "You two! Stop it! You're making a mess." But they don't care. Why would they? They haven't had many responsibilities like the older brothers. They spend most of their time getting into trouble at parties, wrapped up in girl drama. As you can guess, the twin Savin brothers are the hottest teenage boys around New York.

The Savin brothers have always been close, and I admire Mr. and Mrs. Savin for that. They often have big family dinners together. Even when taking vacations, Mr. Savin joins them for a day or two, no matter how busy business is. I'd say they are the model American family, minus the illegal stuff, of course. Whenever I would join them, I felt like I was part of that big, amazing family, and there was a sense of 'home' all around, a sense of belonging.

We're nearly finished with our baked goods, with just a few more left to roll. I can see Mrs. Savin starting to slow down, her hand beginning to tremble. "I'm almost done. Let me take a few more to do," I tell her, grabbing the dough from her. She agrees by giving me a polite nod, wiping her hands on her apron, and then standing back to give me space.

A few years ago, while on a hunting trip, Mrs. Savin was almost asleep when a terrible fire broke out in the house. She awoke to the bedroom filled with acrid, swirling black smoke, coughing and struggling hard to breathe. She managed to get out in time, collapsing on the front porch, spitting up her lungs, which she continued to do for weeks.

She cut her hand open on a piece of glass and got a few burns escaping, too. Mr. Savin spent a lot of money fixing the scars, but the nerve damage couldn't be repaired. While the Savin men were away fighting the cartel, my mom and I sat silently by her bedside so she wouldn't have to recover alone. It was a reminder to us women that we weren't safe. No matter how much security we may have around us, our lives are at stake every day.

The warmth of the oven hits me, as well as the sweet aroma as the door opens, and I can't wait to taste all the things we've made. I excuse myself upstairs to start getting ready for the party.

Room after room, I admire all the decorations, making my way to the stairs. It seems beyond belief that this house will be mine one day; it's so big. I guess I should be thankful, but I prefer my little cottage we left in Seattle.

Once I reach Andrei's room, I close the door, drowning out the noise from the house. Each of the brothers has their own bathroom in their rooms, so I can get ready without running into anyone. It doesn't take me much time to prepare myself, having opted for a simple black dress. My long hair flowing down my back will go well with a shimmer of makeup.

My phone vibrates. Andrei has texted me that he'll be home in an hour. This gives me a few minutes to pack, so I pull my suitcase out from under the bed and add a few more items. Tomorrow, when Andrei leaves for the city again, I plan to catch a flight home to Seattle. Lost in my thoughts, I don't realize Mrs. Savin has knocked on the door until I look up to find her standing in the doorway, leaning hard on the frame as if holding her up.

"You're leaving?" she asks, her voice chilled with disappointment.

"Please don't tell him," I beg her.

"Can I ask why? I thought being with Andrei was what you wanted?"

She walks into the room, stopping only a few inches from me. My body begins to shake by her sudden closeness. Mrs. Savin has always shown me kindness like a daughter, but Andrei is her pride and joy, and she does not take kindly to those who wish to harm him.

"I love him. But I don't belong here. I never did," I answer, my voice shaking, pleading with her.

But she must understand I'm not like the other mafia women, not caring about the money or the power. I want something for myself, and that's what writing my books gave me, independence. Growing up, I wasn't like the other Coalition girls trying to be bosses or marry one. I'd sit in the corner, tuning out the bullshit of this life. Sure, I was born into it, but it's not able to define me.

She reaches out to me with her hand, grabbing mine. I flinch in response.

"Oh, sweet child, do you think I would just pick any little girl to marry my firstborn, the future of this family? I picked you because you were different. You may not want this life, but you were born into it and understand it. Men like Andrei and his father are bad and do awful things. It's easy for them to get lost in this world and become the devils they believe they are. But what sets the Savin men apart is they come home to wives who love and support them. We are their reminder that their priority is family, not power or money. We are the real bosses of this world."

She softly kisses my forehead, and she offers me a soft smile. In some way, she understands me.

"The men should be home shortly. Finish getting ready for the party," she mandates, her voice drifting away as she leaves the room.

Chapter Forty-Five

ANDREI

"Hurry before someone finds us," Cora pleads with me in a low voice.

"Fuck, Cora, I'm turning twenty today. I'm a fucking stallion. I need more than two minutes," I growl as my cock thrusts inside of her.

After the party started, I laid eyes on her and that pretty tight black dress she was wearing tonight. Without a second thought, I dragged her into the chef's pantry, slipping her dress up her ass. I didn't give her the chance to escape before fucking my gorgeous fiancée against the wall.

Both of us moan softly as right outside the door is a kitchen full of caterers preparing the food. I should have picked a room that locks, but security saw us slip in here, and they'll end up on the other side of Nikolai's fist if they let anyone catch us.

Ugh, she's right, though. I do need to hurry as I have important people in my home that I need to catch up with, but her tight pussy feels so damn good.

"I love being your fuck slut!" Cora says, completely surprising me. My only response to her dirty words is the cum shooting inside of her.

A year ago, Cora was a virgin, but the more comfortable she gets about her sexuality, the more she's been letting out a little dirty side of her. I don't want a whore for a wife, but I do like a wife who does whore shit. *And boy, does she do some whore shit!*

I take a few minutes to kiss and cherish her before exiting the pantry. Opening the door, I peek into the kitchen before slipping out. Cora follows closely behind. Casually, I walk past the pastries the women made today and grab one. The sweetness of the sugar melts in my mouth. I kiss Cora on her forehead to thank her before entering the pit.

"There's the birthday man," the newly elected mayor proclaims as he raises his glass to me.

Valentin walks over, joining us with two fresh glasses of vodka and handing me one. The other men around the mayor raise their glasses, shouting, "Happy Birthday!"

I've been meeting with the mayor over the past year, forming a relationship between him and the Savin family. My father usually takes care of the 'political' side of the business. Still, he's insisted I learn during this recent election. After vouching for him, our family, and partners—such as Valentin—also made sizable contributions to his campaign.

Campaign donations are like insurance policies in our line of work. You make payment against a potential guarantee of some future favor.

"You did a great job with this one," the mayor grovels to my father, intending to get more money from us now that he's won.

"I had plenty of help." My father pats Valentin's back.

That's all the ass-kissing I can take from a man who's supposed to be the leader of our city. I only vouched for the son-of-a-bitch because I knew he could be easily bought. I excuse myself to find my 'friends' and use that term loosely.

"Andrei!" a bunch of men my age begin shouting, each holding shot glasses in the air. I'm immediately handed one, the liquid burning my throat. Sasha and I grew up with these guys, the 'elite' group of men in New York, the ones you'll want to know if you're looking for power and money. They're the sons of billionaires, senators, ambassadors, and organized crime leaders.

I've grown up with the guys since grade school, and we've partied until graduation.

We tell stories of college, throwing in some party tales from high school. Growing up, the same kids went to the same parties. We kept our circle tight, allowing a few celebrity kids to join in on the fun occasionally. Especially the pretty ones. The guys are hollering, telling their tales with their stiff cocks pressed against their pants.

"I saw that pretty fiancée of yours," one of the guys blurts out with a slur. He must be drunk to be stupid enough to mention Cora to me.

"I can't believe you ended up with the book nerd," another one laughs. "I thought she was untouchable because she was Sasha's sister. If we'd known you wanted to fuck her, maybe she wouldn't have been off limits in high school." The other guys join in, laughing.

Before anyone has anything else to say, I grab him by the neck, my fingers pressing into his skin. "You will not disrespect my fiancé, do you fucking understand?"

"Yes! Yes! I was just fucking around like we did in school," he wails with his voice shaking, then shrugs me off him.

"Boys, is everything all right?" Valentin asks, walking over to our part of the room. Looking his way, I realize most party guests have stopped conversing to watch us.

"Just having fun, Mr. Volkov," one of the other guys says, rubbing his fingers through his hair. "Let's do another round of shots." The guy passes the bottle around. I don't stay for another round, walking away and bumping into Sasha and my brothers.

"Want me to handle that?" Nikolai snarls.

"It's handled," I tell him. The last thing we need is a wealthy finance tycoon's son turning up in the Hudson River.

"I hate those motherfuckers," Sasha grumbles under his breath.

"I know." My lips form a half smile. Sasha attended the same school as us, mainly because my father paid for him and Cora. Mr. Belov didn't have the bank account balance for Sasha to be part of the group, but because we were friends, the guys opened their arms to him. But he's nothing like them. Sasha is a 'working' man. He prefers to be the one getting his hands dirty than sitting behind a desk. That's what Mr. Belov never understood when he was forcing Sasha to take over his business.

"Boys," my mother calls out, approaching us, the photographer tripping over people a few steps behind her.

We were expecting this. Our mother loves to take family photos at these events.

She grabs my shoulder as each of us rolls our eyes. "Okay, come on, guys," I reluctantly agree first. My mother mouths a 'thank you' to me, her arms flailing around, calling all her children together. We move into my father's office, where there's room to take pictures. This room is always off-limits at events. Oh, and so is the basement where we store enough weapons for an army, our armory being stashed behind a hidden wall in the wine cellar.

Our father is the last one to join. At my mother's request, Cora went out to find him and pull him away from his business associates.

My mother chooses the fireplace as the background yet again. Each of us boys stand over our mother, even at her above-average height. I stand next to my father as the eldest, and Nikolai is next to me as he's not close to our mother. Dmitri always stands next to her as her favorite. And the twins by Dmitri as the youngest. *Same picture, different day.*

The photographer signals us where she wants us to look, asking us to smile, as always. Before she clicks the camera shutter, my father stops her. "We don't have all the kids in the picture," he says, waving Sasha and Cora to him.

Sasha's and Cora's faces light up as they join us. I move Cora between Nikolai and me, and Sasha stands tall behind us. I wait patiently as the photographer snaps so many pictures that I lose count of how many times the flash blinds me.

I look around at my family; the moment is perfect. My life is perfect, too. It's surreal, this feeling of happiness. But my father shortens the family moment by kissing my mother and grabbing his cell phone.

"You're leaving?" I ask him.

He pulls me into the corner of the room. "I'm going back to the city to meet Valentin. We want to deal with the recent threats tonight."

"Then I'll come with you," I tell him.

"No." He stops me, placing his hand on my chest. "This is your birthday party. You need to mingle with our important guests."

"I'll go with him," Sasha joins us. Sasha has wanted some time with my father to plead his allegiance to our family, so it's not a bad idea.

"Call me as soon as you know something," I instruct Sasha.

"Happy Birthday, son. I'm proud of you," my father expresses, heightening my moment of happiness. I hug him and enjoy my father's comfort for a minute, the same as in any family. Tonight is the best birthday I've had.

Chapter Forty-Six

SASHA

The frigid night air hits me as I exit the helicopter, rushing to the waiting vehicle. Mr. Savin and I take the back seat. His security operatives jump into the car behind us.

I place the clip into my weapon and hold it in my lap as we head to the port. We received intel that a gathering of Coalition men will be there tonight. Valentin is on his way to the warehouse, and we'll be about twenty minutes behind him.

"You boys happy to be home?" Mr. Savin asks me.

"Absolutely!" It was no secret that I hated Seattle, all the action being in New York. "I go where you and Andrei tell me to go," I explain, confessing my allegiance to him and his son, emphasizing we are one.

I muster a faint smile, looking out of the dark, toughened glass at the city lights, taking in the world I call 'home.' I remember arriving in the States from Russia as a little boy. The busyness and loudness scared me as I hadn't seen so many people before. But with my new best friend, Andrei, he showed me all the city's cool places, and we made it our playground. Over the years, we began seeing the city as something we owned and belonged to us.

My pocket vibrates. I don't retrieve the cellphone because I already know who it's from. Amy's appointment was a few hours ago, and she's been texting and calling me non-stop since then. I already know what she will say, but I'm not ready to hear it.

A few minutes later, it vibrates again, backed up with a phone call.

"Someone really wants to get ahold of you. Maybe you should answer it." Mr. Savin's voice cuts through the silence.

I slip my sweaty palms into my pocket and answer Amy's call. She fills me in on the details of her doctor's appointment. "I'm busy right now. I'll call later, and we'll talk more about this," I quickly hang up the call.

I shrug, still staring outside, watching the streets and the buildings passing by. We're headed to meet our enemies, and I don't need this distraction right now. This is why I didn't want to get close to a girl.

"Is everything okay?" Mr. Savin inquires.

"Just girl trouble." I slip the phone back into my pocket.

"They never go away," he comments and casts me a soft smile, patting my knee with his hand.

Mr. Savin has been a father to me more than my own blood. Later tonight, I'll confide in him and seek his advice about Amy, but right now is not the right time.

Mr. Savin's phone rings, and he answers it, placing it on the speakerphone. "Get back to *El Grande*," Valentin shouts over the line.

"What's going on?" I grab the phone from him.

"It's a setup!" Valentin's voice drifts off, followed by a click and silence on the other line.

"Motherfuckers!" Mr. Savin calls out.

I immediately direct the driver to get to *El Grande*.

"Call my wife," Mr. Savin yells at me, placing a clip in his gun. I begin to dial her number, but a large bang sounds before I can press the call button, and our vehicle starts spinning. The only thing I can do is hold on to the handles to prevent myself from flying around the back seat.

I hear the tires skidding against the road surface, screeching until the vehicle flips over. My head hits the crushing roof until our car flips again, finally coming to a stop.

I grab my chest, now bruised by my seatbelt.

"You okay, son?" he asks me at last, shaking his head as if to try and stay conscious. I give him a grunt. It hurts too much to talk, and I feel so disoriented.

Lifting my head, there's a view of the driver in the rearview mirror, blood flowing from his forehead into his closed eyes. *He's dead!*

Twisting my neck, I try to catch a glimpse of the vehicle following us, the one carrying our security. I can't see it, but I assume they're with us because there is gunfire outside. Bullets hit the vehicle's frame but don't penetrate the metal. All of the Savins' vehicles are fully armored and bulletproof.

"Stay here," Mr. Savin orders me, gripping the door handle to leave. I grab his arm to stop him.

"No!" The Brigadier is too important to run out into a blood bath. "I'll go."

"It's your job to take care of my son now," he offers before he can open the door. A flash bursts into the night, and my ears are pierced by a pitch so high I think my ears are bleeding.

The window shatters, a shard of glass cutting into my cheek. I grip my face and shield the remainder of it from flying glass fragments.

There's a popping sound next to me. Mr. Savin aims his weapon outside of the door, firing round after round until his clip is empty.

I join him, firing rounds while he puts a new clip into his gun.

Men have gathered outside the vehicle, all aiming their weapons at us, firing straight for us.

I squint, aiming at the man right in front of me, firing two bullets into his face. But when he falls to the ground, I'm not quick enough to shoot the man right behind him, who takes aim right at Mr. Savin. He manages to pump a round into Mr. Savin's chest, sending his body slumping down into the seat.

"No!" I scream, jumping over the seat and placing my body over his. *He can't be dead. Please, God, let him just be hurt!*

The door is ripped open. A man stands right before me, his gun aiming toward me. Quick as a flash, I lift my arm and pull the trigger. The clip is empty.

Knowing defeat, panic takes over, my eyes shooting about the environs, scanning everywhere, hoping someone is around to help. No one is here but the enemy.

"Traitor!" the man says with his piercing gaze, showing his hate for me.

I swallow and take a breath, knowing what will happen next. There is nothing past the barrel of the gun. Then follows the loudest bang and a massive ricochet as my body slams back. My flesh absorbs the shockwaves, vibrating at the point of entry.

***

The ice crunched under my boots, and I gripped the ball in my hand harder. "Cora, where are you?" I called to her in a low voice.

"Here," her soft voice called back to me from behind the tree. I turned to run to her when a hard, compacted ball of snow hit me across the chest.

Turning the other way, I saw Andrei holding another ball in the air.

Cora ran from across the field to the stack of snowballs. "Get him, Cora," Andrei screamed out to her. She held the ball in her hand, deciding who to throw it at.

"You better not. I'm your older brother," I reminded her.

"By twelve minutes," she teased, throwing the ball my way, but I ducked before it hit me.

"You're going to get it!" I charged her. She took off running but was no match for me. Andrei trailed me. I pushed her to the ground, her body hitting the pile of snow softly. Instead of getting up, she began to wave her arms and legs. "What are you doing?" I asked her.

"Making a snow angel," she cried out in laughter.

"An angel just like you are," Andrei muttered under his breath.

I rolled my eyes in disgust. Gross!

It was the first time the Savins had invited us on vacation with them. I lay between my twin sister and best friend, all of us making snow angels. We talked about our futures for hours, and we were happy together. That was the first time I thought that all I needed in this life was the two of them.

***

The memory begins to fade, and I find myself back in the vehicle, shot. I can't find air to suck in. It's as if I'm suffocating. Movement surrounds me, but it's impossible to make out anything with my blurry vision. The night has become ten times more chilling, a frost nipping.

I can't speak. My mouth won't move to say the words.

I need her! Where is she?

My body won't move. *I don't know why. I want to go home!*

When I think of home, I think of them. *Are they safe?*

Another loud bang. My chest feels like it's caving in, as if my bones are so brittle that they're shattering into fragments, exploding within me.

I know it's the end. I know I'm about to have a drink with Lucifer.

With my last bit of hope, my lips finally move to whisper, "Cora."

Chapter Forty-Seven

ANDREI

They say I look like him, both of us over six feet tall with similar physiques. Our skin is darker than that of most Russians. We both display a manful, gritty stubble over a flinty jawline. His dark-brown eyes were stiff and tense. The only feature I got from my mother was her hazel eyes, but we both have the same stare that pierces right through another person's gaze.

I have wanted to be just like him since I was a little boy. He was tenacious and confident but always fair. He welcomed a challenge of his actions and emotions but didn't react quickly. Every move he made was calculated and for a reason.

I look down at the picture in my hand. For my thirteenth birthday, my father took Sasha and me to a New York football game where we watched our team win from the suites. The best part was when my father introduced us to a few players afterward as he talked to the general manager, an associate of his. It was one of the best days of my life growing up. My father had been flying in from Russia all night to take us to that game.

I drop the picture, pick up the bottle of vodka, and bring it to my lips. I have no idea how long I've been sitting here curled up on the floor in the corner of my father's office. I've lost track of time since finding out my father and Sasha were ambushed.

The phone ringing breaks the silence. I answer it, knowing it must be Valentin.

It is, and he sighs on the other line before his cracked voice speaks. "Everything is taken care of. Our friends at NYPD are closing the case as an attempted kidnapping and robbery of one of the city's richest businessmen."

"Thank you," I mutter before hanging up.

I take another swig of the drink. After the initial shock of hearing about their deaths, blame has been hounding me, the sense that I should have fought my father's desires harder and should have gone with him in place of Sasha. Maybe I could have saved him.

It should have been me dead, not them. *I'm a coward!*

I've been hiding in the office to avoid my family, who look to me for comfort but don't know how to give it to them. Waves of strong, intense emotions consume me. One minute, I feel angry. Angry at the men who did this. Angry at myself. I am angry at my father for putting himself into this predicament and at his desertion of us.

The next minute, I am a scared little boy, having cried more today than in my entire life. That is why I can't see my family, unable to give them hope when there is none in me.

I'm not my father. Yes, I want to be like him, but he's too strong a force for me to follow in his footsteps. I thought I'd be ready when the time came for me to take his seat as Brigadier. If you had asked me before today, I would have said I was ready. It would have been wishful thinking, make-believe. Now, without him, I doubt myself, doubting the man I am.

Being Brigadier was going to be an experience I had with my best friend, Sasha. With him by my side, we could have ruled the world. But now he's gone too, so the world we sought to rule has abandoned me.

My chest tightens, and I swallow hard, trying to hold back more tears, though God knows I've shed enough already. I take another sip of vodka to help make me numb.

How can I survive this? Right now, I don't care. I just long to sit here in the dark until I'm too drunk, too stiff, and too cold to feel anything.

Chapter Forty-Eight

CORA

Lifting my numb body, I perch at the edge of the bed, then gaze toward the window to see the darkness has taken over. How long have I been lying in bed, numb to the outside world? At least after hours of crying, I finally fell asleep. A small consolation.

Andrei's side of the bed remains untouched. I haven't seen him since the early morning hours when we received a call from Valentin confirming the deaths of Sasha and Mr. Savin. I didn't need confirmation.

When the birthday party was over, I was so excited about what was next, teasing Andrei about a new leather lingerie set I had bought and heading upstairs to give him his birthday present. Then, a sudden feeling hit me, weird and uncomfortable, as if I had lost something precious.

Andrei was only a few steps behind when his phone started ringing. Instantly, I knew it was about my twin brother.

I slip my cold toes into a pair of house slippers beside the bed. The house had become freezing. Pulling the sweater over my shoulders, I wrap my arms around my chest before leaving the room. It's quiet, too quiet.

Looking down the hall, I see Mrs. Savin's room and wonder if she's sleeping or perhaps softly crying into her pillow. A few tears cascade down my cheeks.

Throughout the day, screams were heard from her room.

The boys have been trying to comfort her, but their hugs can't help, no matter how many they give or how tightly they hold her. She has lost her husband, the man she's loved and been in love with since they married at eighteen. I feel sad for her, sighing already at the thought of being her one day, mourning the loss of Andrei.

As I walk through the hall, very few sounds can be heard throughout the boys' areas. Dmitri and the twins have hidden themselves away in their rooms, feeling helpless.

Brigadier Valentin has ordered all of us to stay here for our safety. Only Nikolai has jumped on the helicopter to head back to the city, intent on leading the Coalition's Army in finding the men who stole everything from us last night. Knowing that the men who shot my brother to death will soon be tortured and killed won't bring any ounce of happiness back into my life.

Before leaving, he came to me. My crying was so loud as I shoved my face far down into the pillow I didn't hear him enter. Feeling the mattress dip, I thought it was Andrei until his big hands roughly brushed the hair from the side of my forehead.

I hadn't realized I needed someone until that moment. It should have been Andrei, but he was too broken himself to offer me anything. Slowly, I sat up with teary eyes and climbed into Nikolai's vast arms. I don't know how long he sat there saying nothing, just rubbing my back as the stream of tears fell onto his chest. Tucking me back into bed, he brought his mouth to my ear and promised me, "I will always protect you as if you were my twin. I won't let Sasha or you down."

And then, he left. The numbness came right back.

Downstairs is empty except for the many security guards posted outside the windows and doors. They hide their faces, trying not to stare at me as I pass by. Coalition men loved Mr. Savin, and their eyes show much sadness.

I stop before entering Mr. Savin's office, Andrei's office. Pressing my ear to the door, I hear nothing but know he's in there.

Gripping the door handle, I push it, but it doesn't open. He has locked himself in there, the very same thing I long to do myself. I don't bother to knock because Andrei would tell me to go away. I walk through the hallway, grabbing the office key. I've been around long enough to know where the Savins hide keys around the house. When I open the door, a sudden sadness overcomes me when I locate my Andrei sitting on the floor in the corner of the room.

"Kitten, go away," his cracked voice mutters.

Shutting the door behind me, I ignore him.

"You can't see me like this. Go away!" He turns his face in the other direction. It's too late. I already saw his swollen eyes.

I crawl on the floor next to him. With my knees tucked into my chest, I lay my head on his shoulder. Just being close to him feels good. I needed him more than ever today. Then, a little guilt hits me. I needed him, but he also needed me.

Mrs. Savin's words replay in my mind. *We are the real bosses.* Andrei has just lost his dad, his idol, and his mentor. It's my turn to be strong for him, to be his savior, irrespective of whether I am weak too.

I grab the half-empty glass from his fingers. The heavy scent of liquor fills the air, and it's obvious he's drunk.

"I need that," Andrei slurs, trying to grab the cup.

"You need to be sober in the morning," I tell him, moving the cup out of his reach.

His eyes look into mine. His gaze is otherwise empty. I cannot lose him, too, especially now that it's only the two of us. We need to let the grief rage through us with its full force if we are to process it. I need to give him that. But we're Coalition, and we grieve differently than others.

Before I can think of what I'm about to do, the palm of my hand hits him across his face.

"Did you just hit me?" he asks, rubbing his cheek.

I surprised myself. But honestly, he needed to be slapped. I need him to be the man he can be, the one his father would want him to be. "Get up!"

He squints his eyes at me but doesn't respond. He turns his head away again, but I quickly grab his chin, forcing him to look straight at me, grasping his face the same way he's done to me many times when I have been stubborn.

I shout, "You are the Brigadier! Not the *future* Brigadier. Get up!"

His eyes bore into mine, wild and enlarged, filled with fear.

"Andrei! We need you. I need you."

His forehead leans against mine. Our eyes are closed as we find calmness in each other's presence. "Do you think I can do this?" he whispers with uncertainty.

"You can do this, and you will do it. Your father believed in you, and I trust him." Mr. Savin raised Andrei to be a Brigadier. He invested everything into the man sitting on the floor, scared.

"I need Sasha."

"I need him, too. But he's gone, and all we have left is each other. So, whatever comes at us, we do it together."

"Together," he agrees, pressing his lips against mine.

Andrei looms above me, extending his hand to help me up. I watch as he strides over to his desk and grabs his phone. "Dmitri, get the helicopter ready. We're going to the city." It gives me some comfort to see Andrei sobering up and barking orders.

As for me, the sun will rise tomorrow, and I will have to start living again with half of me gone.

Together. Sasha would want Andrei and me to stick together.

Chapter Forty-Nine

ANDREI

Man after man, each coming up to my brothers and me, giving condolences. My father was a prominent, well-respected businessman in New York, and there's an endless number of wealthy men here to pay their respects, including the mayor. My mother even received flowers from the Governor's office, personally signed by him. None of them were his real friends, only businessmen who played golf, smoked cigars and talked about how to make themselves richer.

That's how this world works. You never really know who you can trust, and I don't trust most of the men I'm exchanging smiles with right now.

None of us boys could bear standing in front of our father's casket talking about our father, so Valentin has given our father's eulogy. My father would have wanted it to be him.

I stand here alone, looking at his casket, swallowing down a hard lump. I will not cry. There are too many eyes on me now, watching and waiting to see if I show myself capable of living up to the man they all admired.

A friendly hand touches my shoulder, and Valentin whispers, "Ready when you are."

I place my hand on my father's casket, giving him one final goodbye. After we leave, his casket will be lowered into the ground on top of Sasha's. We are burying them together so that Sasha can continue to protect him as they battle hell side by side.

"I'll see you at dinner," I tell Cora, giving her a quick kiss.

She doesn't respond, standing there with a blank stare. She's heartbroken and lost without her twin. I hope my next move will bring her some comfort. It's something that simply needs to be done.

The scent of yellow pine wood fills my nostrils as I stroll through the lumber yard, making my way toward the warehouse. I pause just before the door, taking a moment to gather my thoughts.

"You, okay?" Dmitri asks me. A futile question if ever there was one. No, I'm not okay. An hour ago, we buried both our father and childhood best friend. I don't know if I'll ever be okay again.

Yesterday in the Boardroom, the Pakhan named me as the new Brigadier representing the Savin family. The entire Coalition was in attendance, except the three men waiting on the other side of this door. With a deep breath, I exhale before opening it.

Three Coalition bosses sit in the middle of the room, arms tied to its armrest. They are all that's left of their crew. Nikolai and the Coalition's Army have killed anyone associated with them.

Their wives we left alone, but without much to their names. My hacker drained all their offshore accounts and bankrupted all their legit businesses, leaving their families destitute.

I don't need their money, having too much already. Instead, I distributed their fortunes across the Bratva to buy the other leaders' loyalties. With enough money, men are easily persuaded to turn a blind eye when you're killing one of their own.

I argued with the Pakhan that we had a right to end these men since they are the ones responsible for killing my father. Close friends to Mr. Belov, they too are afraid of the changes I have planned for the Bratva, terrified by how strong the Savin family has become now that we boys are all fully grown.

I step in front of the tied-up men, next to my uncle. The Pakhan never gets his hands dirty personally, but he made an exception here as my father was his good friend and brother-in-law.

The quietness of the room gives a sense of uneasiness as everyone is waiting for me, watching what I'm going to do next. There's nothing to say to these men and they have nothing to say to me. The Pakhan hands over his gun, placing the metal in my fingers. With a tap on my back, I know it's time. Time to end this.

I stand in front of one of the men and signal for my brothers to join me. Dmitri, Nikolai, and I stand tall in front of the enemy, their eyes still full of defiance despite knowing where they are headed. Bratva men don't beg even when they know their lives are about to end.

I point the weapon and squeeze the trigger, a crack of the gun filling the air before the bullet sinks into the man's forehead and his head falls back. My brothers by my side each fire a bullet into the other two men.

Standing there, I take in the moment. They ended my father's life and now, I have ended theirs.

Satisfied, the Pakhan wraps his hand around my neck in a friendly hold, the grin on his face telling me he is proud of me.

Valentin jerks his head to the door. Our job here is done. He and his men will clean up the scene and no one will know what happened to the dead men in front of me. No one will care either, except their wives.

I leave the warehouse just as angry as when I walked in. Killing them has not helped my grief. None of this will bring him back; my father is forever gone.

Chapter Fifty

ANDREI

I dreaded this moment the entire ride from the city. The moment I stepped out of the helicopter onto the grass, I looked up to the sky, praying to my father to give me his strength.

The house is still heavily guarded by our men, but I had asked that they stay away from the inside of the home. Over the past week, I hadn't known what to say to my mother to offer any comfort. The only thing I can give her is space so that each day, she can take a small step into accepting she's now a widow.

But even if you're raised in the mafia lifestyle, you can never be prepared to lose your husband. This is why I must do what's needed to protect my family, so that Cora will never have to go through this tragedy herself. Somehow, Coalition wives carry on believing these hideous things happen to other women's men, never to their own.

Hesitating, I step into the foyer, immediately noticing something new. Our family picture from my birthday party has been mounted on the wall with pride of place. I understand now why my mom desperately craved to capture our family at every event. She knew each one could be our last, even if she never admitted to herself that this could ever become a reality.

The photographer did a great job capturing the moment. We look happy together. I was happy.

Dmitri and Nikolai have entered the house before me. I already hear them joining my mom, Cora, and the twins in the formal dining room. With my chin tucked into my chest, I slowly make my way to join them but the chatter falls silent as I enter the room.

Each of their eyes follows me as I cross the room to take my seat. Not the one I've sat in for the past twenty years, but my new seat as the head of our family.

Slowly, I push the chair out and sit as stiff as a board, bolt upright. My eyes glance up to meet my mother's, and the sight of me in her deceased husband's chair brings tears to her.

Maybe it was too soon to have a family dinner, but it was my mother who insisted we all had to be together tonight. My father would have wanted it, she said, reminding me he was a family man more than a Brigadier.

We had family dinners much more than my friends did with their families. No matter what else we had planned, when my mother organized a family dinner, we all made it a priority to attend. It mattered to my dad, and it meant a lot to us kids, especially since he would set aside all his work obligations just to be there for us and give us his full attention.

I clear the lump in my throat, pick up my fork with jittery fingers, and take a bite. My family too begins to eat the special Russian-themed dinner our chef has made in my father's honor.

One of the lessons my father taught me was that being head of the family often means doing hard things. This is definitely one of them. I'm not trying to replace him and can never live up to the man he was. But I do have to start protecting my family and to do that, I must give out some orders on what is to come.

I was raised to become the head of my family one day, and I have been ready for it. I am ready for it, just never imagining this day would come so soon. I turned twenty barely a week ago, and now I am responsible for my mother, four brothers, and a future wife.

I had imagined celebrating becoming Brigadier with Sasha, the two of us downing a bottle of vodka together and smoking the most expensive cigars we could buy. All that is no more.

Later I'll hide in my office and take that drink. I'll smoke that cigar, look at his picture and toast to my second-in-command.

My brother Dmitri now sits to my right. I know he would love nothing more than to replace Sasha and rule by my side. He probably expects it, but that job will always belong to Sasha.

I look at my brother, knowing this will pain him, but it's the right thing to do. It's part of the plan, my father's plan, and one I intend to execute today.

"What day does school start?" I ask Dmitri. "Are you looking forward to it?" As the smartest brother, he's been accepted into the best colleges in the country.

I catch him by surprise, the way I anticipated. "I thought I would be staying here to help you."

"You will go to college as planned," I say sternly, so there's no room for argument. Before he protests, I add, "It's what Dad would have wanted."

I need him by my side expanding our businesses and making sure our financial position stays strong. But, to do that, he must first go to college and complete his education.

Nikolai has shown immense strength in war. With me as Brigadier, I will ensure he is the right choice for Colonel Lev's replacement. "Nikolai, Colonel Lev is leaving for Russia tomorrow. You will join him." I know my brother won't disagree. He loves training with our Army.

I've already made a deal with the Colonel and Pakhan to promote Nikolai to a leadership position. To be a great colonel, you must know more than how to kill a man. Nikolai has the tactical experience and knowledge of war to elevate our Army to the next level. Under Nikolai, I want an Army that could take out a Navy Seal team if that's what I ask of them.

My plan for Nikolai is to make him so feared that just the whisper of his name brings men to their knees. I add to Nikolai, "The twins will join you until their semester begins again."

The twins sink into their chairs. So far, they've been able to avoid any responsibilities. At the age of fifteen, it's time for them to start contributing to this family. Like the rest of us, they have been trained and are expert shooters. On graduation from high school, they'll work for Nikolai.

I am no longer a college kid in Seattle. It was nice to have that alone time with Cora, but my current role no longer allows me to be selfish with my time and responsibilities.

The weight of our family's success and wealth now rests on my shoulders, and I know it will take a tremendous amount of effort over the next few years to uphold it. With our father gone, our enemies will try to break us, testing our youth. But they will be defeated. The Savin brothers' bond is strong. Together, we will rule the Bratva if for no other reason than because that was my father's plan. He intended to make his sons the most famous organized crime brothers in the Bratva and the world. I intend to make him proud.

Men will try to kill me, and I will kill thousands in the upcoming years. But if I am to try and keep my sanity and not lose myself to this lifestyle—not forgetting why I'm doing it, which is for the love of my family—then I will need her.

Cora sits next to me. She's been quiet tonight. Each day, I watch her battling to become stronger, whole again without her twin.

She hasn't left me yet, and because of this, I trust—or hope—she has no plans to do so. I noticed the suitcase under the bed and at one stage, she was planning to head back to Seattle. With Sasha gone, I can't blame her if she leaves, though it will destroy me.

"Walk with me," I say to her, beckoning for her to follow me.

Chapter Fifty-One

CORA

The flowers glisten in the night's beauty, but I can't help noticing even the flowers have begun to die with the sorrow that plagues this home.

I lean into Andrei's chest, feeling the chill of the air against my skin. As he wraps his arms around my shoulders, we stroll together until we reach the water fountain at the center of the garden.

Since his father's death, Andrei has been distant. I notice his efforts each day to check on me, but his mind seems elsewhere. He often gazes at the wall, his expression tight with frustration and sorrow. I can't imagine the pressure he must be facing.

We stand facing each other, my eyes looking up at him, waiting to see why he's asked me out here.

"Are you happy here with me?" he asks me.

I hesitate to answer at first. Sure, I am happy to be with Andrei, but there have been too many deaths in the last year, something that weighs negatively on our relationship. "There's been a lot of bloodshed," I answer him truthfully.

His fingers fold into mine, and I feel the metal on my finger slip off. My heart stops momentarily when I realize he's taken off my engagement ring.

"Andrei!" I gasp, seeing my finger now bare of the precious metal.

"Things have changed," he says before slipping the ring into his pocket. "I'm not going to force you to marry me because of a promise two dead men made to each other."

I turn away from him to hide my tears. We said *together*. Did that not mean anything?

All the feelings of the past year come crashing down on me. I love Andrei and always have. Being with him is everything I ever wanted. So, when I finally had him, why did I make excuses for us not to be together?

My heart stops. I suck in the air around me to catch my breath. It hurts. The boy I love no longer wants to marry me.

He's the only boy I've ever wanted, and my inner voice is plaintive and bereft, crying out into the air. *Please! I can't lose the man I love!* But when I turn to face him again, he's no longer standing, and my eyes look out at the garden.

The man I love is down on his knees, bending before me with a ring between his fingers. "Marry me, Cora? Marry me because you love me. Marry me because I love you."

Chapter Fifty-Two

CORA

JUNIOR YEAR

The intricate detail of the building is a sight to behold when, in today's world, everyone is designing in a modern flat tone that is just so boring. My eyebrows furrow as I watch the students enter and exit the building on the first day of the semester. I'm ready to return to college, but I already miss Seattle.

After Sasha's death, Andrei strongly supported my decision to spend time at our cottage. Alone there in my thoughts, I was able to use writing to understand my grief and to begin penning my second book.

The more I stayed busy, the less time I had available to curl up on the couch thinking about Sasha, something which has only led to an endless number of tears.

I will never forget him, but as time has passed, I have learned to live without him by my side.

Andrei has been visiting as much as he can but has to spend most of his long days here in New York, taking over the Savin businesses and proving himself as the new Brigadier.

Each day, evil flows through his veins. The Savin brothers are making a name for themselves as the powerful and ruthless men who will someday control the Bratva.

All the men who sided with my father are dead. The men who killed my brother and Mr. Savin ... they too have been slain. Bratva men worldwide are learning it's better to be loyal to Andrei than face the barrel of Nikolai's gun.

Seattle has hidden me from all the bad things Andrei has had to do, but it is time to come home to my new reality. I've been looking forward to coming back to school. The writing program here is among the best in the nation, and I look forward to this year's classes.

Class starts in a few minutes, but I take my time approaching the building, enjoying each hot sip of coffee. My other hand swings freely, but as I make my way to class, I jump in shock when strong fingers slip into my palm. I smell his intoxicating pheromones before seeing him.

"Andrei, what are you doing here?"

I look over to the man standing next to me. Andrei is dressed in a full black suit, looking as if he's about to attend a meeting to close a million-dollar deal instead of going to a college classroom. I glance behind me to find two security guards only a few feet away.

The students passing by try not to stare at us, but their eyes dart our way as they tiptoe around the sidewalk.

Andrei has the appearance of a dangerous man, and he wears it like a badge of honor, showing no concern for how intimidating he seems.

"It's the first day of class." He looks down at his watch and adds, "And we are about to be late."

I wasn't expecting him to join me this semester. He's far too busy to add college classes to his already heavy schedule. "You're coming back to school?"

"I'm a CEO of a billion-dollar company. Men will expect me to be a college graduate when doing business with me, wouldn't you say?" He chuckles softly. Most men who do business with Andrei choose to do so because he's a Brigadier, not a graduate.

I pick up on his humor. It's important for us to 'pretend' we're regular people living in New York's one-percent society.

Our college experience has been unlike any other, no matter how much we try to blend in. What I thought was a way to find myself and gain some freedom from the Coalition ended up with me discovering my real path. You can't run from your past or your responsibilities. A little at a time, you find yourself and realize those things make you who you are.

Being promised to Andrei doesn't prevent me from finding my own path. It just meant I had to become the woman I am and fulfill my dreams differently than most women. In short, it means doing things the Coalition way.

We begin to climb the stairs to embrace the junior year of college, Andrei pausing as our feet hit the last step. Every year of college, someone has died. I pray to God that he gives us the strength to survive this one. "Together," I tell Andrei, nudging him toward the door.

With that boyish smile, the same one I fell in love with the first day we met, he agrees, "Together, Mrs. Savin."

www.ingramcontent.com/pod-product-compliance
Lightning Source LLC
Chambersburg PA
CBHW020415110726
47899CB00006B/1995